BRYSON'S TREASURE
BROTHERHOOD PROTECTORS WORLD

LINZI BAXTER

Copyright © 2019, Linzi Baxter

This book is a work of fiction. Names, characters, places and incidents are products of the author's imagination or used fictitiously. Any resemblance to actual events, locales or persons living or dead is entirely coincidental.

© 2019 Twisted Page Press, LLC ALL RIGHTS RESERVED

No part of this book may be used, stored, reproduced or transmitted without written permission from the publisher except for brief quotations for review purposes as permitted by law.

This book is licensed for your personal enjoyment only. This book may not be re-sold or given away to other people. If you would like to share this book with another person, please purchase an additional copy for each recipient. If you're reading this book and did not purchase it, or it was not purchased for your use only, please purchase your own copy.

ALSO BY LINZI BAXTER

White Hat Security Series

Hacker Exposed
Royal Hacker
Misunderstood Hacker
Undercover Hacker
Hacker Revelation
Hacker Christmas
Hacker Salvation

Nova Satellite Security Series
(White Hat Security Spin Off)

Pursuing Phoenix
Pursuing Aries - March 31, 2020

Immortal Dragon

The Dragon's Psychic
The Dragon's Human
The Dragon's Mate - February 25, 2020

Montana Gold (Brotherhood Kindle World)

Grayson's Angel

Noah's Love

Bryson's Treasure

A Flipping Love Story (Badge of Honor World)

Unlocking Dreams

Unlocking Hope

Unlocking Love - May 2020

Siblings of the Underworld

Hell's Key

Hell's Future

Hell's Vacation 2020

Visit linzibaxter.com for more information and release dates.

Join Linzi Baxter Newsletter at Newsletter

BROTHERHOOD PROTECTORS

ORIGINAL SERIES BY ELLE JAMES

Brotherhood Protectors Series

Montana SEAL (#1)

Bride Protector SEAL (#2)

Montana D-Force (#3)

Cowboy D-Force (#4)

Montana Ranger (#5)

Montana Dog Soldier (#6)

Montana SEAL Daddy (#7)

Montana Ranger's Wedding Vow (#8)

Montana SEAL Undercover Daddy (#9)

Cape Cod SEAL Rescue (#10)

Montana SEAL Friendly Fire (#11)

Montana SEAL's Mail-Order Bride (#12)

SEAL Justice (#13)

Ranger Creed (#14)

Delta Force Strong (#15)

Montana Rescue (Sleeper SEAL)

Hot SEAL Salty Dog (SEALs in Paradise)

Hot SEAL Hawaiian Nights (SEALs in Paradise)

PROLOGUE

Bryson "Ghost" Steele tried to remember his time on the Lazy S Ranch with his brothers, Grayson and Noah. The memories were all that got him through the day. Four days ago, his unit had been captured.

One of his unit brothers had betrayed the team. Ricky Cavous had been using their convoy to run drugs. Ghost had happened to look in the back of the wrong Humvee and found Ricky's blocks of heroin. When he'd turned to tell his captain about the drugs, Ricky had coldcocked him.

When Ghost woke in a cold cell, he wasn't alone. Five men from his unit were chained to the ceiling in connecting cells. Each day, a girl would walk in and pour water down Ghost's throat—enough to keep him alive.

Ghost never saw Ricky. Each day, he heard the cries of his teammates. Ghost hadn't been tortured yet. He'd been hit a few times but nothing compared to what he'd heard from the men in the other cells. Two Taliban men would come in and drag one of his team members out of their cell. He would have to listen to their screams for hours before they went silent. The silence was almost as bad as the screams.

He knew none of his team members would give up the information the Taliban was after. Ghost hoped he could escape. When he did, he would hunt Ricky down and kill him slowly. Ghost felt blood run down his arms from his wrists.

Over the past few days, he'd learned the men's schedule. He was sure the girl who brought him water was sneaking in. She normally arrived right as the sun passed through the opening across from him. The sun had long passed the opening, and night was falling. She wasn't coming.

Ghost closed his eyes for a moment to get some rest, then he heard his cell door open. She'd arrived, and in her hands was a yellowed cup with dirt around the rim. He was sure the water she brought came from a pond. But he was thirsty, and his life depended on it. He needed to survive so he could avenge his teammates.

He focused on the girl. Her hair and body were draped in a long black robe. The only thing he could see was her piercing blue eyes. Judging by her height, Ghost thought she couldn't be older than ten. One of her eyes was bloodshot, and a black rim had formed around it. Anger boiled inside of Ghost.

"Please help me." His voice came out raspy. Even after the sip of dirty water, he wanted more.

She shook her head.

"If you help me, I'll take you away from here."

She stopped at the door of his four-foot-by-four-foot jail cell. "America?"

"Yes, get me that key over on the table, and I'll get you to America. I promise." Ghost didn't care what he would have to do to get the young girl to freedom. If she saved him, he would owe her his life.

When she turned and left his cell without a word, he felt his world crash around him. He wasn't under any illusion that someone would save him. He would meet the same maker his teammates had. Ghost knew he was the last man left. The Taliban might drag his torture out longer.

The jingle of keys brought him back to the present, then the girl returned. She stared at his hands. "I can't reach."

Bryson lifted his dirty feet to her hands, and she placed the keys between his toes. Using his abs, he raised his feet to his hands, ignoring the pain of the chains cutting into his wrists. His body was exhausted, but he had someone other than himself to save now—he needed to save the young lady in front of him. With another grunt, Ghost grabbed the keys from his feet and worked the key into the lock.

When the lock clicked, Ghost dropped to the ground. His body was weak and needed food. His arms were numb as the blood rushed to his fingertips.

"We need to go," the girl whispered as she shook his shoulder. "You promised freedom."

Ghost lifted himself from the dirty concrete. Once he stood, he grabbed the bars of the cell to balance himself. Four days of standing on his tiptoes had done a number on his body.

With a deep breath, Ghost grabbed the young woman's hand and headed toward the only door. When he passed the area where he'd seen his teammates dragged to and tortured, he stopped to grab a weapon. The floor was covered in blood. The horrible stench of decay and urine filled the room. On the table was a set of torture tools, complete with a long knife.

The girl tugged at his hand. "Hurry."

Ghost walked as fast as he could as the young girl pulled him along. He heard voices as they neared the exit of the compound. "Where is everyone?" he whispered.

"Ibrahim al-Asiri is speaking." The leader of ISIS.

Relief hit Ghost as they exited the building, but as long as he was on the streets of Jalalabad, deep in Taliban country, he and the young woman wouldn't be safe. "What's your name?"

"Azadeh."

"Okay, Azadeh, I'm Bryson, and we need to get out of here."

Ghost and Azadeh wove through the streets of Jalalabad. He stole a coat to cover his dirty clothes, and when they were on the edge of town, Ghost spotted Ricky. He was with other troops from the military base. They seemed to be doing a deal with the Taliban.

If Azadeh hadn't been with him, Ghost would've taken the fucker down. When he turned to head in a different direction, Azadeh tripped and cried out as she hit the ground. Ricky and his men spotted them and cussed.

On instinct, Ghost scooped Azadeh into his arms then ran down the street. Gunfire followed him. He felt a bullet hit his leg, but he couldn't stop. He slipped into an alley and hid until Ricky's men ran by. When he felt it was safe, he took off down a side street. A few weeks ago, he'd made friends with a local trying to do better. Bryson ground his teeth and walked through the pain until he reached his contact's house.

Azzat opened the door. "You can't be here."

"Phone. Please let me use your phone."

Azadeh argued with Azzat in Dari until the man agreed to let them use his phone. He wouldn't let them past the entrance though.

"He says we need to leave when done."

Ghost needed to wrap his wound, or he would

bleed out. He tore off a piece of his ragged pants and wrapped his leg while he waited for Azzat to come back with the phone. Ghost hoped he wouldn't call the Taliban. Ghost had saved Azzat's son's life when a fight had broken out in the streets. He hoped Azzat would pay him back. Azadeh stood next to him, making a noise, with a tight grip on his hand. When Azzat came around the corner with a phone in his hand, Azadeh's grip loosened. Ghost hadn't been the only one worried Azzat might've called the Taliban.

Before Azzat could change his mind, Ghost grabbed the phone and called the one person he knew could get him out of his mess.

"Hello." The voice was sleepy.

"Noah, I need help, and I don't know who to trust. I was captured by the Taliban four days ago, and this girl—her name is Azadeh—helped me escape. I owe her my life. My teammates were killed, and the base has been compromised."

Unlike Grayson, who was still oblivious, Ghost had figured out years ago that Noah was in the CIA and had contacts.

Noah let out a slew of cuss words. "Where are you?"

"Jalalabad. Off Chawki Talashi in District One."

Ghost could hear Noah's fingers tapping a keyboard. "Can you make it four blocks? I have a contact at the Afghan Hotel who can hide you until I can get someone there."

"Can you have medical there when I arrive?"

"Yes."

Azzat tapped his wrist, indicating Ghost's time was up. "Thank you, Noah. I'll contact you once I make it to the Afghan Hotel."

Ghost handed Azzat the phone. Azadeh hadn't let go of his hand. She held onto him for dear life. As Ghost reached for the door, an explosion knocked him off his feet. The building crumbled, and the last thing he heard was Azadeh's cry before the world caved in around him.

CHAPTER 1

"It feels like a building hit me," Bryson whispered as he scanned the one-room mud house. His six-foot-four body was stretched out across a dirt floor.

Antonio Ross stood at the door with his arms crossed. "A building fell on you, and if it weren't for Azadeh, we wouldn't have found you."

Bryson groaned as he turned his head to see her sitting cross-legged on the dirt floor next to him, clutching his hand. The young girl's black hair was pulled back, and dirt marred her face.

"That was rhetorical. I didn't need you to actually remind me about the building collapsing." The last thing Bryson remembered was the rocket launcher hitting the building he and Azadeh were in. He'd thrown his body over her to try to protect her from the falling debris. "How long have I been unconscious?"

"You've been in and out of consciousness." Antonio looked over his shoulder for a second. "Two days."

"I need to get back to base and tell them what I saw and figure out a way to get Azadeh out of Jalalabad and back to the US with me."

Antonio opened his mouth to answer when someone shoved him out of the way.

Asher, Antonio's twin brother, walked in. "About time you got up. We have incoming ten clicks out."

"Did you not hear me? I need to report back to base." Bryson frowned.

"I heard you, but as of yesterday, you are officially released from the military. President Tucker sped up your release papers."

"Last I heard, it was going to take a few more weeks for the paperwork to go through."

Antonio shrugged. "The president owes your brother a lot of favors."

"Because he's in the CIA."

"He's no longer an agent either. You're behind on all your current events. We can sit here all day and get caught up, or we can take off before the enemy gets closer." Antonio ran his hand through his hair. "Personally, I want to get back to Fort Lauderdale to see my wife. We were supposed to be on a quick mission when Noah called and asked for us to swing by and pick you up."

Azadeh gripped Bryson's hand. "Don't leave me."

Glancing from the two large men at the door to the young girl, Bryson shook his head. "I'm not leaving you. I will do everything in my power to get you back to the US."

"Bryson…" Antonio ground out. "That won't—"

Bryson held up his hands. "I don't care what it takes. I'm not leaving without her." He glared at his longtime friend.

Antonio looked at the young girl. "We figured you would want to take her, but it's difficult. We'll have to smuggle her out of the country. You have a bounty on your head. Ricky isn't happy you escaped."

Bryson let out a frustrated breath. Azadeh had saved him. He still didn't know how she got him to safety, but he owed her his life. Now she'd saved him twice, once from his cell and again by getting help after the building collapsed on them. "You got my discharge papers through in one day, and you're telling me you can't get her out of the country. Hell, I don't even have a passport."

"We got your stuff, and Noah had a fake passport made for you. It's getting her out of this country that's tricky. I have people who owe me favors, so getting her into the US won't be a problem."

Bryson had saved every cent he'd earned over the years for when he decided to get out. Four months ago, when his dad passed, he figured he'd already missed too much time with his family. The decision to not reenlist had been easy. He was heading home to the family ranch to spend time with his brothers. "I have money."

Asher laughed out loud. "Unless you were doing something illegal for some pocket money, you don't have enough to get her out."

"Well, I'm not leaving without her, so you guys can take off. Thanks for getting me this far. I don't care what you say. I owe her my life, and I'm not leaving without her." Bryson slowly stood. Every muscle in his body hurt, but he was determined to figure out a way to save Azadeh.

"You can barely stand." Asher elbowed his brother. "Lucky for you, your friends have more money than most people in the world."

Bryson frowned. "I can't accept your money." He reached out to help Azadeh stand. "Thanks for helping us this far. We can take it from here." Azadeh wrapped her fingers in his. There was no way he could let her down.

"Don't worry about it. We can take care of the funds." Asher pulled the wood door back and motioned for them to head outside. "We figured you wouldn't leave her, so we worked something out, but we need to leave now."

Bryson glared at Asher and Antonio. "Then why were you giving me grief about taking her?"

"Even with the plan, getting her out of the country won't be easy, and you might not like what we have in mind," Asher muttered.

"I help."

All three men looked at the young girl and smiled. Bryson figured she had the two mercenaries wrapped around her finger from the gentle smiles they each gave her. "Well, are you ready to head out?" Bryson asked Azadeh.

She nodded. That was all the confirmation he needed to walk out the door with her small soft hand in his. Bryson raised his arm to shield the desert sun as he walked out of the hut. Seconds after he walked outside, sweat trickled down his back.

They were in a remote village filled with mud huts. Women and children ran up and down the dirt roads as young boys walked around with guns in their hands. "This doesn't look like any city near Kabul." He tilted his head from side to side, trying to relieve some tension. "How far are we from the Kabul airport?"

"Around a hundred and seventy-five miles." Antonio crossed his arms. "But we're not heading to Kabul. Ricky has men looking everywhere for you, and that will be the first airport they go to. Peshawar's airport is closer and harder for Ricky and his men to reach."

A shiver went down Bryson's spine, hearing his old teammate's name. Bryson had caught Ricky smuggling guns and drugs to the local Taliban. Ricky had locked him up and tortured his teammates for four days before Azadeh had helped him escape. Now they had to cross the Pakistan border with Azadeh and figure out how to get her on the plane with no one noticing.

"Ricky should be on a plane to Guatemala for life in prison," Bryson grumbled as they walked toward the Humvee. "How are you planning to make it across the Pakistan border with Azadeh?"

"We called in a few favors," Antonio said. His longtime friend had been a highly decorated SEAL before he decided it was time to get out. It probably also helped that the president of the United States was a family friend.

Azadeh's grip tightened around his fingers. Nobody would stop him from taking the girl back to the US, but it would not be easy.

For the first time in Bryson's military career, he was more worried about saving Azadeh than making sure Ricky paid. Until he met the girl, the military was everything to him. His choice to not reenlist had been hard, and he was struggling with it each day. Now he wanted to get to the US.

He'd planned to spend some time in Denver with Grayson before heading to Montana to spend time with Noah. Everything had changed the second Azadeh had handed him those keys. She was now his number one priority.

Bryson lifted Azadeh up into the back seat before climbing in next to her. "Are you sure these friends of yours can get us through?"

"If they don't, we have money." Asher shrugged before starting the Humvee. "Enough money always gets you what you want."

Azadeh tilted her head. "Like real family?"

Bryson's heart squeezed for the young girl. "You have me now." He reached over and wiped a wayward tear that slipped from her blue eyes. "You will always have me."

Asher gave him a tight nod before shifting into gear and heading down the dirt road.

Antonio shifted in his seat. "I have a guy waiting for us at customs in Fort Lauderdale. He'll have everything we need to get Azadeh from Florida to Montana."

Denver was where Bryson grew up on the Steele family ranch with his two older brothers. In the last year, both of his brothers had found love in Montana. One still lived there, and the other had gone back to Denver.

"Why Montana?" Bryson asked. "I figured we would go back to Denver and figure out how I can legally adopt Azadeh."

Antonio's jaw ticked. "CJ informed us not too long ago that Ricky has people looking for you in the US. We have fake identification for you. Hank Patterson and his team are also in Montana, and they can help protect you and Azadeh until we figure out how to eliminate the threat."

"I'm not going to put my brother in danger.

Azadeh and I can rent a car when we get to Florida and go into hiding."

"Stop being so dramatic," Antonio huffed. "Your brother is more deadly than most people I know. He hasn't told you guys what he really did in the military, and it's not my place to say, but he can take care of himself, and with the Brotherhood Protectors in the same town, you'll be safe."

"I know he's in the CIA." Noah thought he was the only one of the brothers who had done work outside his branch of the military. There were things Bryson's brothers didn't know about him either. Bryson had seen Noah on an operation a few years back and had put the pieces together.

"Was." Asher's face lit up. "Your brother laid into President Tucker after he completed one last favor for him. We had to hear all about it when the president called and asked us to help you. I believe he muttered that your brother might owe him again. Furthermore, Noah is dating a close friend of the president's. I highly doubt he's out."

Bryson adjusted his body in the back seat. The dirt road did nothing to help his aching back after being tied up for days then having a building fall on him. He rested his hand over his eyes, hoping to get a few minutes of sleep before hitting the border. Asher and Antonio seemed to think it would be easy. Bryson had crossed the border many times, and it was always an issue.

A SOFT HAND startled Bryson from a nightmare. It wasn't his first since joining the Marines, and it wouldn't be his last. He was happy he didn't swing back, as he normally did when someone woke him from his trips down memory lane.

"You upset?" Azadeh asked.

Bryson looked around the Humvee. They were alone, Asher and Antonio stood in front of the vehicle, talking to two armed guards, but they weren't at the border. They had already made it to a private airfield. He had slept through the whole drive, and his body still hurt, maybe even more. The bruise on his side was ugly. There was a ninety percent chance his ribs were broken.

He watched as the guards argued back and forth with the Ross brothers.

Bryson's gun was within reach. He grabbed it off the suitcase in the back and checked to make sure it was loaded. He had no doubt that Asher and Antonito were both carrying, but he wasn't going to step out there without having another gun for backup.

"Azadeh, stay in the Humvee no matter what. If something goes wrong, drive away. Don't stop until you get somewhere safe. Here." He pushed his brother's number into her hand. "Call him for help."

"Won't leave you."

Bryson pinched the bridge of his nose. "You need to stay safe. If it gets bad, leave and call him." He waited for her to climb into the front of the Humvee. Her feet barely touched the pedals, and he felt pretty sure she had no clue what to do. He showed her how to put it into gear and brake.

When he jumped out of the vehicle, he heard the doors click behind him. At least she listened to one of his demands. He hoped if things went south, she would listen to the other demands. As he got closer, he heard the four men arguing in Urdu. Over the years, he had picked up a few words here and there but not enough to understand them at the rate they were speaking.

In the backdrop sat a sleek plane with an AR symbol on the side. Bryson knew it was the Ross brothers' plane, but the guard wasn't letting them near. With each step Bryson took across the tarmac, the conversation got more heated until the two soldiers pulled their guns and pointed them at the guards.

Everything happened so fast: the sound of squealing tires, followed by more shouts, gunfire, and Asher throwing his body into Bryson. Bryson's head hit the hard ground, and everything went black.

CHAPTER 2

"When are you going to find yourself a good man?" Eric Richman grumbled.

It was the same question the gray-haired man asked each time Lynn came into the feed store. He was hell-bent on her finding a man to take care of her. Lynn didn't need anyone to watch over her. Joining a cult taught her that lesson the hard way. Three years ago, almost to the day, she ended up having a bad day and thought joining Faith of the Glorious One would help her deal with her troubles. It wasn't glorious at all. Lynn hadn't realized what she'd gotten herself into at first. When she'd been told she couldn't leave, her hackles had raised, but by that time, it had been too late. She shook her head, trying to stop thinking about the cult.

She smiled back at the old farmer. "I told you last

week, and I'll tell you the same this week: whenever you're ready to take me on a date, I'm game."

"I'm too old for you." He tapped his chin for a second. "But that new man that came into town, now he's a sharp lad. What's his name…? Noah… Noah Steele."

She shook her head. "Noah Steele is happy with Matilda. You know I wouldn't be here if it weren't for him, Matilda, and Hank Patterson. It's going to take me years of doing them favors to repay them for what they did." Shivers ran down her arms as she thought about what might have happened if Noah hadn't broken up the cult before Keith sold her.

"Yeah… I thought I heard someone say something about Matilda having a brother and that's why she ended up here."

Matilda's brother was the sweetest young man in the world. He cared about everyone, and the reason he joined the Faith of the Glorious One was to get money to help Matilda out. Each day Sebastian had made sure everyone was okay. He wasn't like the other men at the facility. Lynn was happy nobody except Keith touched the women without getting in trouble. A few tried, but the women had been told those men were sent away. She knew now that wasn't true. The men were killed along with any women who tried to leave. The police found a burial spot in the back of the land the cult was on.

"He's too young." Lynn tapped the Christmas bell

hanging on the two-foot tree next to the register. "I promise I'll be fine alone."

"Nobody should spend Christmas alone. Rosa and I've spent every Christmas together since we were married sixty-five years ago." Mr. Richman's eyes always twinkled when he talked about his wife.

Lynn hadn't met her yet but planned to soon. She loved to cook, and making Christmas cookies was something she enjoyed. That coming weekend, she planned to make a batch and take them to a few people around town for what they had done for her.

The bell above the door sounded, and they both looked to see who had walked in. It was someone Lynn didn't recognize, but she hadn't been around long enough to know everyone in the small town of Eagle Ridge yet. Mr. Richman nodded to the newcomer as he walked down one of the aisles.

The old feed store was one of her favorite places to go. Everyone wanted to help. Each time she came in, Mr. Richman would give her a different man to go on a date with. He even tried to set her up with his twenty-one-year-old nephew.

Dating wasn't at the forefront of Lynn's mind. She was still licking her wounds because she had caught her husband of three years cheating on her and made a rash decision to join a cult. She didn't need a man anymore. Her vibrator did just fine, and the horses at Brighter Days gave her someone to talk to. There would come a time when she would leave the ranch and start her life over. Lynn just didn't know when that would be.

"I'm happy for you and your wife. Sometimes marriage works out, and sometimes you come home to find your husband in bed with your friend."

"Did you kill him?"

"Nope, spending time in jail for him wasn't on my to-do list, but a stupid self-help podcast was, and I heard Keith Creighton talk about Faith of the Glorious One. Next thing I knew, I was handing him all my money."

"Mr. Creighton should have had a slow, painful death for what he did to you and those other women," Mr. Richman muttered as he curled his lip.

Lynn wanted to move on and no longer think about Keith and the cult. Most of the women in the cult had been young. She was one of the older women and spent her time talking to the girls. Almost every girl in the house had run away from home or an abusive relationship.

She glanced around the old store as the hairs on her neck rose. She felt like someone was watching her. It wasn't the first time she'd had the feeling since the night the Brotherhood Protectors raided Faith of the Glorious One. Over the last week, she'd felt it more often. Unsure if she should tell Taz or not, she'd kept it to herself. Lynn didn't want to bother her boss with it. Taz and Hannah had been kind enough to hire her. Deciding the feeling was her cue to leave, she reached into her pocket and pulled out the check Hannah had written and handed it to Mr. Richman.

The old man meant well, but it was time to head back to the ranch. Lynn loved the cold December days. Last week, Brighter Days Ranch had brought in a rescue horse, and she'd spent almost every free second she had with Midnight. Someone had abused the horse, and he was having a hard time adjusting—the same way Lynn had felt when she came to the ranch.

The guy who had walked in a few minutes before came up to the counter with a stack of rope and a shovel. He was close to her five-foot-eight height and had shaggy black hair. She couldn't see his eyes, because he had glasses on. Something about him gave her an uneasy feeling, and she quickly grabbed her bag and said goodbye to Mr. Richman.

She wrapped the scarf tighter around her neck as she pulled open the door. A gust of cold wind took her mind off the creepy guy. Careful not to step on an icy patch, Lynn made her way to the truck. Once inside the cab, she locked the door and placed the bag on the seat next to her. Creepy dude came out of the store and watched her as he got into a new BMW. Not the type of car she often saw in Eagle Ridge, especially in the dead of winter.

Lynn turned the engine to the old pickup truck and sighed when it started. The heat was on full blast, and she waited for the truck to warm up a little. Fuzzy gloves protected her hands from the cold steering wheel. The area to pick up the feed she'd bought was around back. After waiting for the BMW to back up and leave, she slowly made her way out of the parking spot. Georgy, Mr. Richman's nephew, was waiting by the back door with her four bags of oats.

He had the bags loaded into the truck before she had time to exit. With a wave, the young man walked back inside the feed store, and Lynn turned the truck down Main Street to head back to Brighter Days.

She smiled to herself as she drove down the snowy road toward the ranch. Not a day passed that she missed living in a large city. Everything moved so fast. Time seemed to move even faster, and sadly people didn't stop and get to know each other. Forty days had passed since Noah and the Brotherhood Protectors security team had rescued her. Each person rescued had a loved one to go home to except Lynn. Oh, she had a cheating ex-husband she could have called but nothing else.

Lynn had grown up in foster care after her parents died in a car crash when she was younger. With no immediate family, she got tossed from home to home. Three years before graduating high school, Ms. Jackson took her in. That was where she learned about horses and nature. But Ms. Jackson didn't want her to stay at the ranch the rest of her life. The older lady made Lynn keep her grades up so she could go to college. And as a ward of the state, her college was paid for. During Lynn's last year of college, Ms. Jackson died of a heart attack, and her oldest child took over the farm. Lynn fell into a depression, then along came Gabriel, her good-for-nothing ex. They met her freshman year. His family was rich, but she didn't care. He was a good friend, and gradually they started to date. When they both graduated, he proposed, and she said yes. Looking back, she'd married more because she had no one.

Spending her days with the horses even when the temperature was ridiculously cold gave her more validation than sitting behind a computer all day. It also made her miss Ms. Jackson when she snuck the horses apples. She turned down the back road to the ranch. Snow started to coat the road as she flicked on her wipers. Gripping the steering wheel, she watched the road like a hawk. That week was her first time driving again in three years. Keith hadn't let her leave the compound once she showed up at Faith of the Glorious One.

Taz had driven into town with her the first couple of times to make sure Lynn felt comfortable. With each day that passed, she felt a little more stable. Hannah had talked with her off and on to see how she was doing after getting out. Six FBI agents had interrogated her four hours after the release. Now she felt stupid that she had joined.

It wasn't just that. She'd watched other women come and go. Now she knew Keith had sold them, and Lynn had done nothing to protect them or figure out what was going on. The last list of women who were to go to auction had her name on it. If Noah hadn't shown up in time, she would have become someone's slave. A chill went down her spine just thinking about it.

Motion in the ditch made Lynn's lips twitch. A momma deer and her baby were running through the field. The sight brought back so many memories of living on Ms. Jackson's farm—getting up before school to help Gerald with the fence. They would often see wildlife waking up and walking around. Lynn placed her foot on the brake to slow down. She wanted to make sure she was going slow enough in case they decided to turn and run toward the road, but she couldn't stop. Nothing happened. No matter how hard she pressed on the brake, the truck didn't slow. Her knuckles turned white from gripping the steering wheel so tight. She took a couple of deep breaths and pumped the brake again. Nothing. It seemed the truck was speeding up instead of slowing down.

She stared at the sharp turn coming up. If the road was in good condition, she might be okay taking the turn at sixty miles an hour. But the road was slick from the snow. Survival instincts kicked in as she scanned the area, looking for a way to slow the truck.

She spotted her only option. Noah might not be happy, but she had to go straight down the Steele brothers' road instead of taking the turn. Even with her foot off the gas, the truck's speed kept increasing. She eyed the large trees along Noah Steele's property.

Her only options were to jump out of a moving car or take the tree head-on. No time to change her mind. The turn was coming up.

Everything happened in a matter of seconds. Lynn turned the truck slightly toward the tree, and she braced for impact. It didn't matter how well she braced. Her head flew forward and hit the steering wheel.

Pain shot through her skull, and darkness enveloped her.

CHAPTER 3

"You mad?" Azadeh asked in a soft voice. It wasn't the first time she'd asked the question in the past twenty-four-hour trip across the globe.

Each time she asked, her eyes were glossy with tears, and it broke his heart. He didn't know how many times he would have to tell her it was okay before she would understand he wasn't mad. Concern that she could have hurt herself was the only thing that filled his mind, and that wasn't until he woke up.

Smiling, he reached into his carry-on to grab another candy bar. Bryson knew she couldn't live on chocolate, but the smile on her face each time she ate it made him happy. "I promise I'm not mad at you." He handed her the Hershey's bar. "I didn't mean to yell. I was worried you were hurt, not the guards."

"Bad men." She played with the wrapper before slowly ripping the side open.

Azadeh wasn't the best driver, but she was able to take two men out so they could get on the aircraft. Customs had cleared them to leave, and the plane had been waiting. The guards were trying to get money out of Asher and Antonio. They'd overheard the brothers bribing the customs worker to get Azadeh out of the country. Bryson had no doubts the men would've killed them and taken what they could find. "Yes, bad men."

He glanced around the first-class cabin. It was nice but not as comfortable as the Ross brothers' private plane. In the past, Bryson had only ever flown regular commercial or military. When they'd landed in the private airfield in Fort Lauderdale, customs hadn't blinked an eye at the passengers. Antonio had handed him and Azadeh a set of tickets, and an hour later, they were on another flight.

Azadeh had slept in the bedroom of Antonio's private plane. Bryson, on the other hand, hadn't been able to fall asleep. He looked down at his watch. He'd been up well over twenty-four hours. It wasn't the first time he'd stayed up so long. Many missions called for no sleep, but he hadn't done it in a while. Bryson knew no one on the commercial flight was going to try to take Azadeh from him, but he couldn't turn off his concern. When he got to his brother's, he would crash for a few hours.

Once in Montana, he would call in every favor owed to him to make sure Azadeh's paperwork made it through the right channels. Antonio had already started the process and was sure it wouldn't be long before things were okay. Asher had told Bryson that he had a bounty on his head. Another decision he would need to make once he reached Montana was if he should leave Azadeh with Noah while he worked to take down Ricky and his men. Bryson wasn't going to let the corrupt soldier get away with using the military to move drugs.

As soon as the airplane descended, Azadeh gripped his hand. She'd done the same when they'd landed in Fort Lauderdale. Before yesterday, she had never been on a plane, but she didn't complain or say anything, just held his hand each time they prepared to land. Moments later, the tires skimmed the tarmac, and the pilot turned on the reverse thrust to slow the aircraft down.

He wasn't sure how his brother would take receiving an extra person. Bryson hadn't stopped to tell Noah that Azadeh was coming back with him.

Once the seat belt light turned off, Bryson released his seat belt and stood. Antonio had gotten him and Azadeh the first seats on the plane, so they both stood. Neither had bags or any extra items of clothing. He would need to stop and buy things for her immediately so she would have something to wear to bed.

Growing up, his mom had always talked about wanting a little girl, but it had never happened. Now Bryson found himself taking care of one and had no clue where to start. So far, they hadn't had too much of a language barrier. Azadeh understood what he said, but she struggled with coming up with words to reply.

The stewardess popped the door open, and Bryson reached down and grabbed Azadeh's hand. "Ready?"

She smiled up at him and nodded. They hadn't had time to shower since leaving Pakistan. Antonio gave them clean clothes on the airplane, but he still felt the dirt and sweat on his body. Azadeh's hair needed to be washed. He wiped a smudge of dirt off her face before guiding her into the airport.

The Eagle Ridge airport terminal was on the smaller side. They followed the signs leading them to baggage claim. He expected his brother to be waiting for him. If Noah wasn't, Bryson would need to find a phone and figure out how to get ahold of him. Not taking the burner phone from Antonio was starting to bite him in the ass. The Ross brothers had insisted, but he figured he didn't need it. Bryson pinched the bridge of his nose. He was tired and still in a lot of pain. Twenty-four hours of flying did nothing for his bruised ribs and throbbing head.

Bryson hadn't even had time to think about getting out of the military. For as long as he could remember, he had planned to enlist in the Marines. He looked up to his older brothers and had wanted to be like them. The only difference was that Grayson and Noah went into the Navy. Then Noah had gone to the CIA.

Now, Bryson was getting thrown back into the civilian world. He'd thought he had a couple more months to figure everything out, mostly to look for a job. His talents could be utilized outside the military. Bryson was the tech guy for their unit, and he spent his downtime developing his hacking skills and working on a network security system to stop hackers.

Luckily, he backed everything up to the Cloud. No one knew where his computer was. It hadn't been with the couple of things Asher was able to retrieve. Ricky and his crew must've gone through Bryson's things when they had him locked up. One of the first things he did was build a self-destruct code into his startup. If someone entered an incorrect password three times, the computer would automatically erase the data.

Finishing his product would be his priority. He needed to find a software developer to help with the last few pieces. Over the years, he'd put away a lot of money for when he decided to get out of the Marines. Now he had a young girl to take care of.

Bryson shook his head when he stepped into the baggage claim area and noticed his brother holding a large Welcome Home sign. Next to Noah stood a short woman holding an equally over-the-top decorated sign.

"My brother's over there." Bryson pointed out Noah to Azadeh.

Noah set the sign down and walked a few steps before his eyes landed on the girl next to Bryson. Bryson had to give it to his brother. The look of surprise that washed across his face was quickly neutralized. "Ghost."

Bryson rolled his eyes. "I'm out of the military. You can call me Bryson."

Noah wrapped him in a hug before stepping back. "We called you Ghost way before they called you that at boot camp."

It was true. Bryson ended up with the same nickname in the military as he had growing up, but both times it was given for different reasons. When he was little, he'd thought a ghost lived in his closet. To that day, he still believed the house he grew up in was haunted. In basic, everyone had said he was like a ghost, never could be seen.

Bryson nodded. "Azadeh, this is my brother Noah and his girlfriend, Matilda."

Matilda smiled and pulled her into a hug. "I'm so happy to meet you. I didn't know you had a daughter."

Noah frowned. "He doesn't. I assume you are the

little girl who answered the phone when I called to ask your location."

She nodded. "I answered. Thank you for help."

His brother smiled down at Azadeh. "I think I'm the one who's supposed to thank you. If you hadn't answered that phone, I bet I wouldn't be talking to my brother now." He ran a hand through his hair. "When you called for help, and I heard a bomb, I almost lost it. Thankfully the Ross brothers were close by. I don't know what I would've done. We've lost enough family."

He was right. Their mom dying when they were young was hard, but the death of their dad was even worse. Remorse washed over Bryson. He'd spent so many years going after the next mission and not coming home to see his dad.

Bryson grabbed Azadeh's hand. "Do you have room for both of us?"

"Yes." His brother narrowed his eyes. "I don't know why you would even ask that."

Bryson couldn't help but frown. "It's not that simple. The Ross brothers told me I have a mark on me, and I haven't had time to look into Azadeh much." His gut twisted, thinking about putting his brother in harm's way. "Antonio helped me get her here to the US. He was able to get her a temporary visa, but it's not in her name. She was supposed to be wed to Ibrahim al-Asiri."

Noah let out a stream of cuss words, and Matilda

gave him a questioning look. "Who's Ibrahim al-Asiri?" she asked.

"He's the leader of a radical group and likes to collect young brides. The younger, the better."

"No marry, please."

Bryson dropped to his knee next to the girl. "I will do everything I can to keep you safe, and if that means going on the run, we will. You will not marry that man."

She let out a little sigh and wrapped her arms around his neck. The young girl already had him wrapped around her pinky. She had also saved his life three times now. There was nothing he wouldn't do to make sure she was safe and could live a normal life.

"Let's be clear," Noah interjected. "You saved my brother, and that makes you family." He turned from Azadeh to Bryson. "We're in this together. We've spent too many years fighting alone. It's time we fight as a family."

His brother was right. They'd all been away from each other too long. "Thanks, protecting Azadeh is my number one goal. I'm not sure how long we're staying in Montana, but this is where Antonio booked our flight to."

"We wanted you out here with us," Matilda said as she led the way toward the exit. "Grayson and Kara are settling in at the Steele ranch, but we figured you might still want to work somewhere else, and our friend Hank Patterson is always looking for people to join Brotherhood Protectors."

Bryson opened the back door to the quad cab pickup. "Hank Patterson?" he asked before jumping in next to Azadeh.

"That's him." Noah opened the door for Matilda to climb in. "He has a good crew out here. Over the past few weeks, he's dropped hints about me joining, but I'm trying to put those days behind me and clean up Kara's ranch."

"How is she?" Bryson had heard bits and pieces of the story. He still couldn't believe her own dad was going to sell her for the land. Now Bryson's oldest brother was engaged to a billionaire.

"They came up and helped when we raided that cult to get Matilda's brother out."

"Bryson told me about that. Did all the girls go home?"

Noah sighed. "All but one. She said she didn't have anywhere to go. She wasn't telling us everything, but we worried she would shut down if we asked too many questions." The truck started up, and warm air filled the cabin. "Lynn is staying at Brighter Days for a while. It's a rehabilitation ranch for wounded vets. They also have a really good therapist. Not only was she the oldest one there, she was also kept there the longest."

The hairs on the back of Bryson's neck rose. "Are you sure she wasn't part of the cult?"

Matilda answered his question. "Not one hundred percent sure, but my brother said Lynn helped the younger girls. I think she'd gone through something in her past, and she was going through the motions, not picking up on the clues of what was going on around her."

Bryson rolled his neck, trying to relieve some tension. "Young girls were being sold. How could she not pick up on the clues?"

"Keith Creighton, the leader, is really good at brainwashing people. Taz is engaged to the owner of the ranch. He thinks she feels bad for not picking up on the cues, but she's also hiding from something." Noah went more in-depth about what had happened to Matilda on the way to the Montana Gold Ranch.

Snow fell around them. The light jacket Azadeh had on wouldn't be warm enough for the coming days. December in Montana could get brutal. It would get cold enough in Afghanistan to snow, but nothing compared to what the temperatures could reach in Montana.

"What the hell?" Noah grumbled.

Bryson looked out the window to see an old pickup truck smashed into a tree, but the truck was still pushing the tree. Through the window, he could see someone hunched over the wheel. He threw open the door and ran toward the truck. Dirt filled the air from the tires continuing to spin. The sound of the tree cracking had Bryson's blood racing. If the tree broke, a deep ravine was on the other side. His feet raced against the road. The woman inside was still unconscious when he made it to the truck.

He tugged at the door handle, and it didn't move. The truck was locked. Not sure how much longer they had, he reached for a rock on the side of the road and broke the side window. Glass shattered everywhere, but he didn't have time to think about that as he quickly unlocked the truck door. He pulled the woman as hard as he could. Her limp body fell against him just in time. The tree snapped, and the truck went over the cliff. The sound of crunching metal came from far below, but the woman in his arms was still out.

CHAPTER 4

Hannah, the owner of Brighter Days, insisted Lynn recover and spend some time in the house. She argued with Taz that Hannah was overreacting, but neither of them would budge. After Lynn complained for two days, Hannah finally threw her hands up and let Lynn return to work.

Lynn put on her coat and scarf and practically ran out the door before someone could stop her. The cold Montana wind hit her the second she stepped outside. After being kept in a house for the last few years, Lynn loved spending as much time as she could outside.

Collin, one of the ranch hands, was standing by the pen with Taz and a couple of the horses. She waved as she rushed into the barn toward the back stall. She hadn't seen Midnight since the day of the accident.

Midnight came to the door the second he heard her coming. She couldn't hold back her smile for her favorite horse. She grabbed the carrot out of her pocket and held it out. He practically inhaled the treat. "Did you miss my treats?"

"I made sure I gave him a treat each day. He wasn't as excited to see me as he is to see you." Taz smiled, coming to stand next to her.

"You have everyone spoiling you." She scratched Midnight's ear for a second. "Thank you for taking care of him. I know he's not mine, but something about him clicks with me."

A new ranch hand came running around the corner. "I didn't know anyone was in here." Two seconds later, another man came running and threw a snowball before he saw Taz and Lynn. The first guy ducked in time. Lynn was not so lucky. The snowball hit her dead in the chest. Last week it wouldn't have hurt, but it was right on her bruise from the seat belt.

"I've told you two numerous times not to throw snowballs in here. You could have spooked a horse, and what if we had a stall door open? Go muck the stalls."

"I'm sorry, Lynn." The two boys turned and marched out.

Any other day, she would've made her own snowball and had fun with the two ranch hands. Both men were in their early twenties and close to the end of their therapy. Physically she couldn't see anything wrong with them. Taz had told her they were serving together when their Humvee was hit. Both suffered from brain injuries along with PTSD. They were excited to leave together and move to Arizona to work on a ranch that needed help. Friday was their last day at Brighter Days Ranch.

Hannah was doing great work with the men and women Lynn had met. Taz had asked her a few times to talk. She knew it was only a matter of time before she would need to let them know everything about the cult. Her past before then was not something she wanted to talk about either.

"I think we should take you to see a doctor. The snowball was mostly powder, but you looked like you got punched."

Lynn frowned. "I know my ribs aren't broken."

"So you've had your ribs broken before?"

"Will you drop it if I say yes?"

Taz took a seat on one of the square bales. "Nope."

Lynn had been the one to open her damn mouth a second ago. "I broke my ribs when I was younger."

Taz raised his brows and tilted his head. "You need to give me more than that. I'm worried about you. Something in your life was bad enough to drive you to join Faith of the Glorious One, and you were there for three years, Lynn. That's a really long time to be locked away from civilization. Sebastian told us the women weren't allowed out of the house."

Midnight helped ground her as she petted the

horse's neck. "One of my foster families had a bully, and we were fighting over a toy. He pushed me down. When I landed on the edge of a cement stair, my rib cracked." Lynn held up her hand for Taz to keep quiet. "The boy was immediately removed from the home. A few months later, I was moved into Ms. Jackson's care, and I stayed with her until I graduated."

"Did she have horses?" Taz asked.

Lynn shrugged. "She owned a ranch outside of Seattle. Horses weren't the only animals she raised. Ms. Jackson had a heart of gold and took in foster kids all the time. The ranch was like this, a therapy center for kids who needed help."

Taz nodded. "Is she still running the ranch?"

Lynn wished Ms. Jackson were still alive. She would've run back home with her tail between her legs when she caught her husband cheating on her. Instead she'd joined a cult and had almost been auctioned off to some crazy person.

Brighter Days felt close to the life she knew before going to college. With how technology had changed, she probably wouldn't even know what to do with a computer anymore. Cell phones had already advanced a lot in three years. At the place where she lived for those three years, they had a landline, no cell phone. The only time she'd used it was to make sure the papers she had filed for divorce were taken care of. That was the one thing she did before leaving the state and her crappy marriage.

"No, she died my senior year of college."

Taz frowned. "What did you go to college for?"

"Computer programming." Lynn sighed. Taz wasn't going to stop since he had her talking. "I promise to go get a job soon so I can pay you back for the truck. Not sure how much my degree will help now. A lot has changed in three years."

"You don't owe us for the truck," Taz huffed. "I'm just happy you're alive. Noah sent pictures over this morning. You would've died if you'd stayed in there any longer."

Lynn turned at the sound of heavy footsteps. Her face immediately flushed when she saw the handsome man who had saved her life. She'd come to in the middle of the road after he'd pulled her out. When she'd looked up, she'd gotten lost in his crystal-blue eyes. Everything had happened so fast after that. He'd left without giving her his name.

Next to him was a young girl no more than four feet tall with shoulder-length hair. Her blue eyes held so much pain and bitterness. Lynn didn't need to know the little girl's story to understand she had lived through something terrible. Her little hand gripped the hand of the man who'd saved Lynn.

The man next to him she knew. Noah came over and gave her a hug. "You look pretty good for being in an accident a couple of days ago." He handed her a wrapped plate. "Tilly made you some homemade cookies. She wanted to come over and check on you with us, but she had to run to Bozeman because Sebastian needed something for class."

"Please tell her you didn't have to do that." She peeked under the lid. "Are these peanut butter cookies?" The last time she'd enjoyed cookies was years ago. Not waiting for Noah to confirm, she reached in and took one out. It was delicious. Not wanting to be rude, she offered cookies to everyone. The young girl was the only one to take her up on the offer. The smile on the girl's face from the cookie made it worth sharing.

"I heard you guys had a meeting with Hank," Taz said as he walked over and shook Noah's hand.

"Yeah, that's the other reason we're here."

"Azadeh, why don't you ask Collin if he'll help you pet one of the horses?" the sexy cowboy told the young girl. He wore jeans and a black jacket, and his sandy-blond hair peeked out under his cowboy hat. She couldn't help but stare, and the way he took care of the young girl made her swoon even more.

When it didn't look like she was going to move, Collin walked over and kneeled in front of her. "Hi, Azadeh. My name is Collin, and I know Midnight would love a carrot. Do you want to help me feed him?"

"Okay." She dropped the cowboy's hand and followed Collin out of the barn.

Lynn had a sinking feeling that the men wanted to talk to her. She feared they were going to demand she talk about the cult. Deep down, she knew she should've told them everything. She didn't want to retell the story, because now that she was out and knew about what had been going on, the regret of not doing something to help the others was overwhelming her. All the women who had been sold could've been saved if she had opened her eyes.

"Lynn, this is my brother Bryson," Noah introduced them.

"I'm glad to see you're doing better. You scared the crap out of us."

"Thank you for saving me. I should be the one cooking for you guys. Noah's saved my life twice in one month."

Noah blushed for a second before schooling his features. "I wish we were here just to see how you are doing, but we need to ask you a few questions."

Lynn shifted on her feet and sighed. "I know I need to talk about my time in the cult. It's not easy."

"Cult?" Bryson shook his head. "We aren't here to talk about the cult. From what Noah said, everyone involved is dead or in jail. No, we're here to talk about who wants you dead."

Lynn rolled the word around in her head: dead. She didn't even know anyone anymore. "I'm pretty sure you have me confused with someone else."

The three men didn't say a word. They continued

to watch her. With each second that ticked by, she felt more unsettled.

Laughter bubbled up. They were serious. They thought someone wanted her dead. "I'm not sure why you think someone would want me dead. It's not like I've talked to anyone in the real world except a few people at Brighter Days and the feed store. Mr. Richman seems to like me and he's not the type to attempt to take me out."

Noah's lips twitched. "I think Mr. Richman would rather have you go on a date. Last I heard, he was trying to set you up. I know we haven't talked about Faith of the Glorious One much. Did we miss someone? Or is someone from your past looking for you?"

"Why don't you explain why you think someone wants me dead? I haven't seen any signs of someone wanting to harm me."

Bryson tilted his head to the side. "The truck you were driving was tampered with."

Taz leaned against one of the stalls. "I know for a fact it didn't happen out here. Someone did something when you were in town."

The man at the store came to her mind quickly, but she dismissed it. Lynn had never seen him before, and she didn't think he was from Eagle Ridge, anyway. The men were making her feel paranoid, but if someone was after her, that put everyone at Brighter Days in danger.

"Can you give me a couple of days to try to find a job before I leave?"

"Why the fuck would you leave?" Bryson shouted.

She immediately shut down before remembering she wasn't under Keith's control anymore. "Because if someone's after me, I'm not putting Taz and Hannah in danger."

"We aren't going to let you leave."

Saying those words to most people would make them feel safe. As someone who wasn't allowed to leave a house for years, she didn't feel the same way.

"I will not be held captive again." She pointed at Taz. "I appreciate everything you and Hannah have done, but you will not hold me here against my will." Her hands shook, and the room blurred from the tears in her eyes.

Bryson sighed. "How about you guys go see how Faith of the Glorious One is doing while Lynn and I talk?"

Taz walked over and wrapped her in a hug. "I didn't mean to make you cry. You can leave whenever you want. Hannah would be heartbroken if you left because someone was after you. Talk with Bryson, and see if he can explain better than me."

The two men left, and she was left standing next to him.

"Come sit with me on a bale."

When she sat next to him, she did everything in

her power to keep her body from leaning toward him.

"Let's start with how we had someone loot at the truck after it was retrieved from the bottom of the cliff. Someone cut the brakes, and how it was done means it had to have happened in town. What Taz was trying to say is we want to help you and figure out who did this. You can leave or stay, but taking off is not the best option until we find the guy who did this."

"What happens if they come after Hannah or someone on the ranch?"

Bryson twirled a piece of straw between his fingers. "I just got here the other day, but without talking to anyone on this ranch, I know they would want to protect you. These men are ex-military. Maybe they got hurt, but their instinct to protect is still there. Are you saying you don't trust them with your life?"

She glared at the sexy cowboy. "That is not what I said, and you're trying to guilt-trip me into staying."

His lips twitched. "Did it work?"

"Yes, but if something bad happens, it's not my fault."

CHAPTER 5

"I LOVE THAT LITTLE GIRL. She's doing amazing with the horses, but you need to get her into a child therapist soon." For the past week, Hannah had talked with Azadeh each day.

Bryson wanted her to settle in. President Tucker had come to the rescue when he helped push her paperwork through faster. Her green card was on its way. When things settled down, Bryson would look into adopting her and officially making her his daughter. He had considered her his the second she'd helped him escape the torture chamber in Afghanistan.

He rested his foot on the stall. Lynn's horse, Midnight, walked over and pushed at his hand, looking for a treat. His lips twitched at the gentle creature as he gave the horse a carrot from his pocket.

"With her paperwork coming in, I feel more comfortable reaching out to someone for her to talk to. Thank you so much for doing it in the meantime. I know a few psychiatrists in Bozeman I plan to call. I'm worried she's hiding the worst of what happened to her. Her parents died three years ago. Her uncle is cruel. I think I should take her to a doctor also, but I don't know how she'll react."

"She hasn't opened up much about her time living with her uncle. She's only talked about her parents and how much she loved them." Hannah shook her head. "And you, she worships the ground you walk on. Azadeh is strong, but if you leave her, she will fall apart."

Bryson narrowed his eyes at Hannah. "I won't leave her."

"You don't need to get your feathers in a bunch. I'm just telling you what I've observed from talking with her."

"Sorry. Have you talked with Lynn yet, or is she still in denial about someone coming after her?" It wasn't necessary for Bryson to stay at Brighter Days while Hannah talked with Azadeh, but he told Taz he wanted to help out around the ranch since they refused to take his money. The real reason was to spend some time with Lynn. He found her doing something new each time he showed up, but he always caught her looking at him when she thought he wasn't paying attention.

Hannah's eyes narrowed. "You like her." It wasn't a question. She was stating the obvious.

"Yes." Bryson glanced out the door where Azadeh and Lynn were playing in the snow. "She's hiding something."

Hannah nodded. "Besides the day we told her she was in danger, she hasn't said anything else about her past." She jerked her head toward the front of the barn, where Taz stood. "I talked with Taz the other morning, and he agrees. If she doesn't open up soon, we're going to take a look into her background. It's not something we wanted to do. We were hoping she would tell us." Her brows drew together. "But we have to think about the men and women at the ranch. I'm not saying we won't help her. We just need to know what we're protecting her from because it's not the cult. Every person is locked up or dead, and if they aren't, her hiding stuff is not going to look good for her."

Bryson narrowed his eyes at Taz. "If anyone's going to look into her background, it will be me." Something about letting someone else look into Lynn was unsettling. He wanted to wrap her up in a blanket and put her somewhere nobody could hurt her.

"Yeah?" Hannah studied his every move. Bryson knew she was looking for something. "You know if she finds out you looked into her background without permission, she might not forgive you for invading her privacy. If we have one of Hank's men do it, she'll be mad at us not you."

"I don't know Hank's computer guy, and I can find the info just as well." There was no way he planned to let anyone else look into her.

Hannah drew in a long breath. "No matter what I say, you aren't going to listen. I've seen the way you watch her with Azadeh. She does the same to you. My advice is to get to know her and let others work on figuring out what's going on. She might be on the shy side, but she has a hidden temper, and if she finds out you dug into her past, Lynn might cut off your balls."

Laughter drew his attention from the conversation to the open door. For a December morning, the temperature wasn't too bad—well, not bad for Montana. Anywhere else it would have been fucking cold out. He watched as Azadeh packed a snowball and threw it at Lynn. A chuckle escaped his lips as Lynn collapsed to the ground, acting like the snowball had taken her out.

The ranch reminded him of the one he'd grown up on outside of Denver. A tall shed stood in the background, filled with tractors and other farming equipment. Next to it was a long bunkhouse for the employees at Brighter Days. "How long do most of the patients live here?"

"They aren't patients," Hannah growled. "They're

guests, and until they're ready to leave. Each person takes a different amount of time."

Bryson nodded. "You're doing an amazing job with this place. I wish more people would do things like this."

"Hospitals and therapy work for some, but unless the soldiers can get out and do things, they start to get into their own minds."

"After my dad died, I realized how much time had passed since I enlisted. Grayson called to say he and Noah were getting out. I knew it was time to start thinking about it. The only thing for me is that it happened quicker than I originally planned. I wanted to have work lined up. When everything with Azadeh is settled, I'm going to have to find something."

"I'm sure Hank Patterson has a job for you, if you wanted. From what your brothers said about you, he would hire you in a second."

Noah and Grayson hadn't even heard about all his missions. Bryson had taken on many missions that weren't even on the books, some led by Ricky, and now he wondered how much of the mission was for the government or for Ricky to line his pockets. "I'm not sure if that's what I want to do. My background is IT, and Hank already has one on his team."

Hannah snorted. "I wouldn't be surprised to see you and your brothers open your own company one day. If I was a betting woman, I'd say a slew of people owe you and your brothers a million favors."

She was right. Bryson had called in quite a few of them to get everything lined up for Azadeh even with President Tucker's help. He didn't want her to be in the US illegally, and he had the correct papers now. At first, he worried she could be tracked with her name. Bryson didn't know when, but he figured her uncle would come looking for her eventually. Each night he looked to see if someone had placed a reward for someone to find her. The same bounty for his head stayed on the black market: fifty thousand dollars, dead or alive.

"Honestly, with everything going on, we hadn't talked about it. I know Noah is enjoying fixing up the ranch, and Matilda is working her butt off with him. Grayson and Kara are back in Denver, so I don't know how we would work anything out."

Midnight pawed at the door to his stall. "You're not getting enough attention?"

Hannah snorted. "Lynn slept in that pile of hay right there last night. This horse is spoiled rotten."

They kept the barn heated, so it wouldn't have been that cold inside.

"She does that often?"

"Almost every night," Hannah replied. "I catch her talking to him a lot."

Bryson wanted Lynn to talk to him. He glanced out the window in front of the barn and watched as Lynn and Azadeh continued playing. The sudden urge to be with them came over him. He laid a carrot in the palm of his hand and held it out for Midnight. The horse quickly ate the carrot and licked his hand, wanting more. Bryson patted him on the neck before turning toward the exit.

Hannah walked behind him as he reached for the barn door and pulled it open. Azadeh looked his way when he stepped outside, and she came running toward him and wrapped her arms around his waist. He couldn't help but smile down at the little girl.

"We were having a snowball fight."

With each passing day, the hollowness in her blue eyes went away a little. Every so often, he would catch her staring off into space, and the haunted look would return. He knew she would need more sessions with a therapist. Bryson could only do so much, but the time at the ranch had seemed to help.

Lynn stood a few feet away with her hands in her pink snow jacket. Her long brown hair was down with a matching pink hat covering part of it. The slight wind had made her cheeks pink. "Azadeh has a good arm."

"I used to carry water for the younger girls so they wouldn't get in trouble."

Nobody spoke. This was the first time she spoke about what happened when living with her uncle. She had been too young to carry water when she lived with her parents, so she had to be talking about her time with her uncle.

Bryson cleared the emotion from his throat and

reached down and playfully squeezed her arms. "Wow, you do have guns on you."

"I not carry a gun. Only the boys carried a gun."

He ignored the gasp that came out of Lynn's mouth. "No, we call muscles in your arms guns. I was talking about how strong you are."

"Okay. Me not want to carry a gun."

Bryson wrapped his arms around the young girl and pulled her in tight. Over her head, he watched Lynn quickly wipe tears from her eyes. "I promise you won't have to carry a gun."

"Even if Uncle comes for me?"

"He won't." Bryson would die before he let anyone take her away from him. If he had to, he would go back to Afghanistan and take care of her uncle himself. The thought had already crossed his mind a couple of times.

Bryson was so focused on the girl, he hadn't noticed Hannah leave. He was alone with Lynn and Azadeh. Lynn must have also noticed Hannah was gone.

"I had fun playing today. Maybe tomorrow you could help me brush Midnight."

"Yes." Azadeh ran and threw her arms around Lynn. "I help."

Lynn raised her brow. "I'm sorry. I should've asked you first if you even had time to come back tomorrow."

A smile danced on Bryson's lips. "We'll be back tomorrow, but we also don't have anything going on right now. Azadeh is having so much fun already. Do you want to show us how to brush the horses?"

"I would, but I have to take a few supplies out to Percy and Vasquez. They're working on the fence." She tilted her head to the side. "You guys could come with if you know how to ride a four-wheeler. I bet Taz would let you use his."

He looked at Azadeh. "You want to take a ride on a four-wheeler?"

"Four-wheeler?"

Bryson pointed over to the ATV and watched Azadeh's face light up. "Yes!"

The three were heading toward the ATVs when Bryson heard horse hooves pounding against the cement. Midnight was the only one in the barn, and Bryson knew for sure he was locked up and Hannah had headed toward the house.

Lynn must have heard the same things because she looked back at the barn right as Midnight plowed through his closed door, splintering the wood into a million pieces. The horse's eyes were wild. Something had spooked him, and there was no stopping him.

Midnight was headed straight for them, and Lynn wasn't moving her feet. She called the horse's name, but he didn't slow down. The horse was picking up speed as it got closer. The thud of his hooves hitting the ground grew louder.

"Run to the house, Azadeh." Bryson didn't have to ask twice. Azadeh took off, but Lynn wasn't moving. Without thinking, he threw his body at Lynn to knock her out of the path of the horse. He twisted in midair so, when they came down, she landed on top of him.

Even with snow covering the ground, it didn't do much to break his fall. When his back hit the dirt, the wind was knocked out of him. The bruise on his back hadn't healed from his time overseas, so it added an extra layer of pain.

Midnight ran by and stopped near the fence with the other horses. Lynn had been seconds from being run over. Her eyes were wide as she looked down at him. When she shifted, he couldn't help but groan and not from pain. She rubbed against him, and with each movement, he got harder.

Her pink tongue ran across her lips. "Thank you."

"Anytime, darling."

She hadn't moved, as his arms still held her, and she looked into his eyes. The world around them disappeared. He wanted nothing more than to press his lips against hers.

"Are you guys okay?" Taz asked.

Lynn quickly climbed off him, but Bryson needed a few minutes to get his body under control.

"Yeah, something spooked Midnight." She was already halfway across the yard, going to get the horse.

Something had happened in that barn, and Bryson was going to figure out what it was.

CHAPTER 6

Lynn wrapped her fingers around Midnight's halter. His nostrils flared as he breathed. Whatever had scared him must've been bad, but Lynn's heart was racing for another reason. "I almost kissed him," she whispered into Midnight's neck.

She'd felt his erection press against her as she moved around on top of him. It had only added to her need. She'd gone three and a half years without sex. One time lying on top of his very hard, muscular chest, and her woman parts were going haywire.

"Here." Bryson came up behind her and handed her a lead.

Midnight nuzzled against her as she clipped the lead onto his halter.

"Thank you. He still seems spooked."

Midnight tossed his head and let out a neigh. She ran her hands down his neck, and Midnight pawed at the ground. Taz came out of the barn with a grim look on his face. Whatever had spooked Midnight wasn't good. Collin walked out next with a burlap sack, and when it moved, Lynn knew it was a snake.

With her stomach in knots, she headed over. "Let's find out what they found in the barn."

"Taz and I found a rattlesnake in Midnight's stall, but someone also unlatched the gate. When we looked at the video feed, it was blank. I know we locked the gate when Bryson and I were in there. We need to figure out what's going on. It seems to be directed at you, Lynn."

Midnight nudged her shoulder, trying to get her attention.

Bryson reached over and grabbed the lead from her hand. Azadeh walked over and slipped her little hand into Lynn's. Azadeh looked up with her blue eyes. "Bryson and I protect you."

Lynn couldn't help but smile down at the young girl.

She watched as Bryson led Midnight over to a pen. She didn't miss the twitch of his lips when Azadeh spoke. "I'm not sure who would be after me. How can we be sure it's me they're after? A snake could have wandered in."

Bryson came back and stood in the circle next to Azadeh. The young girl hadn't dropped Lynn's hand, and she felt the girl shiver for a second. They had been outside in the snow for a while, and it was time to talk about her past.

"Everyone around here knows how much you love Midnight, and the stall door was left open. If it had been any other horse, it might not have been related, but the camera feed was turned off. Someone is trying to mess with you."

"Well, it's not going to work," she insisted. For too many years, she'd let people run all over her, and they weren't going to run her out of the one place where she'd started to feel like her old self. She wasn't completely sure who the old Lynn was, but it wasn't someone who was going to run at the first sign of danger. Lynn looked up at Bryson. He'd clenched his jaw at her statement.

"Whoever is messing with you made a move in the middle of the day with everyone around." Bryson pointed at the wiggling burlap sack. "Whoever did this is getting desperate to come after you with everyone around," Bryson huffed.

She glared at the snake. "I don't know who would be after me. It wasn't like I was in the barn."

Lynn's mind was racing. She had no idea who she could have made mad enough to do such things. Hoping they would just go away wasn't an option. "I don't think it's someone from my past. I only know one person who fits that bill, and I have no clue why he would come after me now."

"Let's go inside, and you can tell us who you think

it might be." Bryson motioned toward the house. "If you tell us your real last name, we might be able to find more info."

Her cheeks turned red from the lie she'd told Taz and the police. Over the past few weeks, Taz hadn't said a word about it. She knew he had kept the cops away and told them she would talk to them again when she was ready.

If she was being honest with herself, she would never be ready to talk about her past, but it was time to talk about her ex. She didn't think he would try anything, but someone was coming after her.

"Okay, but I need something strong to drink." She turned and walked toward the house.

She sat down on the couch in the living room, and Azadeh sat right next to her. Bryson sat on Lynn's other side. Taz and Collin sat down on the two chairs, and Hannah came and sat on Taz's lap.

Bryson reached over and squeezed her leg. "Nobody will judge you here. We just want to help."

Closing her eyes, she rested her head against the back of the couch. "My current last name is Rockefeller. Five years ago, I married Gabriel Rockefeller." Lynn felt Bryson pull away from her at the mention of being married. "Three years ago, I received an offer from a well-known company for an app I developed. I accepted the deal and sold the app for over a million dollars. When the deal was done, I wanted to celebrate with Gabriel, but he traveled a lot for his position in the family industry."

"Just want to make sure I'm clear on this. Are you talking about the Rockefellers who own RRT Consulting?" Hannah asked.

"Yes, his family owns that company, and everyone works for them. One of the arguments we had for years was that I wouldn't work for them or develop any apps for them. I wanted to keep my work life separate. I kept it a little too separate, I guess."

"Why haven't you tried to contact him yet?" Taz asked.

Lynn let out a long sigh. "Give me a second. I'm trying to get there." She paused for a moment to collect her thoughts. "After I sold my app, I was so excited, I booked a flight from Seattle to New York to surprise him and tell him about what I'd done. It was me who ended up getting the surprise. I walked in on him with another woman."

Bryson and Taz didn't need to know it was their mutual friend since college. That was when the dark cloud had come over her, and everything had felt like it was falling apart. "After Ms. Jackson died, I looked for something to fill the void in my life. Looking back on my relationship with Gabriel, I married him to help with the void and nothing else. We had no love in the relationship, lust maybe. Nothing more."

She had longed for a family, and once Ms. Jackson died, she lost the little family she had, so when

Gabriel had proposed, she thought they were going to build a family. Then she found out he didn't want kids. She decided she was okay with just the two of them. Even after she caught him and her friend together, she considered staying with him, but on the flight back to Seattle, she heard a podcast by Keith Creighton and decided it was time for a change.

His promise was what she'd been looking for: working to become a better person while having a family to surround them—something she had wanted ever since her parents died. Ms. Jackson had helped to fill that void for a long time before she passed, but it hadn't been the same.

"What did you do?" Bryson asked.

"I left New York and headed back to Seattle. That's when I heard about Faith of the Glorious One. Gabriel kept calling, trying to tell me it was a mistake. I knew he didn't slip and accidentally put his dick in her."

Taz coughed to cover his laugh.

Lynn continued the story. "I went straight to the penthouse, cleaned out my things, and went to a hotel."

Most people would think finding their husband sleeping with another woman would be the worst part of the story, but it wasn't even close. "I need a drink to get through the rest."

Hannah nodded, rising from Taz's lap, and headed toward the kitchen. It was a little past noon, so at least she wasn't morning drinking. Azadeh still had Lynn's hand wrapped in hers. The little girl was amazing and such a bright light in the room for such an ordeal. Lynn had lost her family at a young age, but the girl had gone through so much more.

It wasn't long before Hannah walked back into the room. She handed the two men beers and Lynn a glass with amber liquor. She was thankful for the hard liquor and not the beer. With a quick gulp, she downed the glass in one swallow.

"The next day I met with a lawyer and filed for divorce. I didn't want anything from him, so the divorce was quick. I signed the document and sent it to him to send back to my lawyer. Once I signed the documents, I called and spoke with my lawyer. He said everything was final."

Bryson tilted his head. "Did you get the signed documents back?"

Lynn shrugged her shoulders. "He had no reason not to sign. I didn't ask for anything, and per our prenup, I could've had millions. The only thing I wanted was the money from my app sale."

He took a sip of his beer. "But you don't know if he signed them?"

Taz opened his phone. She watched as his fingers tapped away. His brows furrowed more each second. Lynn hadn't turned on a computer since she'd escaped with the other women from Faith of the

Glorious One. Every so often she would watch the local news but nothing more.

Taz cleared his throat. "I'm not sure the divorce went through. There are reports saying he's looking for his long-lost wife and a couple of videos of him pleading for you to come back home. Holy shit, he has a ten-million-dollar reward out for you."

That couldn't be right. "No, he signed the documents. Why wouldn't he?"

She didn't expect anyone in the room to answer the question. Nobody would know the answer. She still couldn't believe he hadn't signed the papers. She couldn't fathom why he would make a video looking for his lost wife. Nothing made sense.

"There's something you aren't telling us. It's better if you get everything out, and we can figure out exactly what we need to do to help you."

"After I sent the divorce papers, I went to live with Keith and his cult."

"That's it?" Bryson asked.

"No, my fee to live there was a million dollars. I was the reason he had the money to traffic all the girls, and I didn't pay attention to what was going on around me. I sat there and did nothing to help those girls. The past three years, I was so wrapped up in my own sorrow and feeling bad for myself."

"Not your fault." Azadeh squeezed her hand. "We make mistakes."

Lynn couldn't help but smile down at the young

girl. She was too embarrassed to look in Bryson's direction. Matilda's brother had ended up at the cult because she had given the funding to keep it open.

"It is my fault. None of those girls would have left their families if it weren't for me and my money. I think the only reason Keith took me in was because I gave him so much money. They took men of all ages to help keep the women in line. Women were never older than twenty-one. Looking back, I feel like such a fool for what I did."

Bryson reached over and squeezed her other hand. "Keith knew how to use people. If you hadn't given him money, he would have gotten it another way. Now that we know what happened, we can get you out of this. First, we need to work on getting rid of that ten-million-dollar reward. If I had to guess, I bet someone recognized you and wants the money."

"But she almost died. Why not send Gabriel information about her location?"

"We protect you." Azadeh smiled up at her. "Come stay with us."

Lynn didn't know how she could be in the same house with Bryson. The man was sexy as hell, and she was still married. To a man she hated more than anything.

"I agree." Bryson looked at Taz. "I think it would be better if she stayed with us because someone knows she's here. Let's not tell anyone she's coming to Montana Gold Ranch. I'll work on figuring out what Gabriel's endgame is."

"Do I get a say in any of this?" She didn't like anyone making decisions for her.

"Yes, you can decide, but we can help you. Let us help."

She couldn't say no when she looked into his eyes. "Yes."

Azadeh let out an excited squeal next to her. She couldn't hold back a smile at the young girl's excitement.

CHAPTER 7

MARRIED. He rolled the word around in his head. She married into one of the wealthiest families on the West Coast. The Rockefellers had old money, more money than he could ever dream of having. Azadeh saying Lynn should come live with them was a good idea. He just didn't know how he was going to be with her around all the time. She was so beautiful, and he always wanted to reach out and touch her. Earlier he'd thought she was going to kiss him when he'd plowed her to the ground.

Now they were in his brother's truck heading to Montana Gold Ranch. Noah had agreed with the plan even with the Brotherhood Protectors at Brighter Days. It would be safer to move her without anyone knowing. Bryson planned to look through all the info on her husband and figure out what he was really after.

"Are you sure this is the best idea? I planned to save up some money at the ranch and then find a way back to the city for a paying job. Not sure if my skills are very useful anymore. I haven't used a computer in three years."

Bryson couldn't wait to hear about the app she'd developed. He had never been a fan of programming, but that didn't mean he wouldn't like to hear about it. Computers had to be the least romantic thing possible to talk about. Hopefully, it would keep his mind off her beautiful body and on the task of saving her from whoever was trying to scare her.

Montana Gold Ranch was owned by his future sister-in-law. It wasn't very far from Brighter Days. He turned down the long gravel road toward their destination. Azadeh had come to love the place in a short time. Each morning she would get up before him and Noah and wait downstairs until it was time to go out and help with the animals. He knew she loved to work with them, but something more was going on. He thought she felt she needed to help to keep her place in the house. All Bryson wanted was for her to be a kid, something she hadn't been able to experience since her parents died.

Noah had bought two of the trained rescue horses from Brighter Days Ranch. Hannah and her team of guests had done a fantastic job with the horses. Bryson would talk to Hannah in the coming days to see if they could bring Midnight over to the ranch as well. Since learning she was still married, Lynn had shut down, and the sparkle he'd seen in her eyes earlier was gone.

"What was the name of the app you sold?"

Lynn's cheeks turned pink. "The company didn't use the actual app for their store. They took the back-end code and combined it with their app."

"Do you like writing code?" Bryson asked as he turned down the long gravel road toward the ranch.

"I love a good puzzle, and to me, code is like solving a puzzle. Each piece has to line up perfectly, and when it does, you have a masterpiece."

"I never thought about it that way. Over the years, I've written scripts to help me get by but never a huge chunk of code."

"What is code?" Azadeh asked from the back seat.

"Has Bryson let you play any games on his phone?" Lynn asked.

On the flight from Afghanistan to the US, when she woke, Antonio had given her an iPad to play with. Bryson had downloaded a couple of games she could play, and when he'd arrived in Montana, Noah had handed him a new phone, and he'd added a few more games for Azadeh. He didn't want her playing them all the time, but he'd found a few to help her with English.

Azadeh smiled from ear to ear in the back seat. "Yes! I'm on level two."

Bryson looked in the rearview mirror. "I don't

want her to get hooked on the games, but I felt like learning English was a good game."

Lynn tapped her finger against the armrest. "Those games can be very helpful. Azadeh, those games run off a bunch of words and other symbols, and that is what we call code."

"You write video games?" Azadeh asked.

"No," Lynn said. "The code I wrote helped with an algorithm inside an app. My code made it easier for the company to offer more merchandise to the consumer based on their browsing history."

"Can I ask what company you sold the code to?" Bryson inquired.

"Simonson Expomed Inc.," Lynn said. "The more I think about it, I could've gotten a lot more for the code. I was so excited someone wanted my work that I didn't even try to negotiate. They sent the contract, and I accepted seconds later without even reading the fine print."

"Are you going to work on developing another idea?"

"Not sure." She sighed. "Three years is a long time to be away from technology."

Bryson glanced over at Lynn for a second. "Things change. All you can do is try."

Lynn nodded. "I feel like my life is in turmoil and I will never get off the hamster wheel. After finally getting out of the cult, I thought I could start over and not have to talk about my past or what I did. I knew I couldn't stay at the ranch forever. That place is for wounded vets who need help."

Bryson gripped the steering wheel. "Your giving Keith that money didn't change the outcome. Stop blaming yourself. It's not going to do any good. If you hadn't given them money, someone else would've. A few years ago, I met Lexi, and she was a cruel b-word with deep connections. She would've found another way to do what she was doing."

Lexi was a rogue CIA agent using her connections to help Keith sell the girls around the world. She was also the one who'd found many of the girls they'd sold.

"I know that in my head, but I can't seem to communicate the same thing to my heart." Lynn shrugged. "You're right. Lexi is a cruel b-word. Somedays I think the underground prison the CIA sent her to will be too nice."

"It's not." Bryson rolled his neck. "Two years ago, I had to drop off a few terrorists to the location. The cell Azadeh rescued me from was the Ritz-Carlton compared to what those men and women have to stay in."

"You were captured?" Lynn asked with worry in her voice.

"Yes," Azadeh added from the back seat. "But I helped get him out of the cell."

Bryson smiled back at the young girl. "Azadeh

saved my life over in Afghanistan, not once but three times."

"Wow, Azadeh, you're an amazing young woman, and now I understand why Bryson wanted you to come to the US with him. I know it's only been a week, but did you get her papers?"

"President Tucker fast-tracked her citizenship." He would be in debt to the man for the rest of his life. "Everything is in order, but I worry because her name is out there. Her uncle won't be happy I took her."

"Uncle is bad," Azadeh chimed in from the back seat. "Oh, look. Noah has a kitten."

Bryson parked next to the barn, where his brother stood with a little kitten bundled in his arms. Azadeh loved playing with the cats out in the barn, and each day, she checked to see if the momma cat had given birth to her litter.

She tore out of the truck when it came to a stop and rushed toward Bryson's brother as fast as her legs would go.

"Do you want to go see the kitties?" Bryson asked Lynn.

"Yes, I'd love to." Lynn reached over and rested her hand on his forearm for a second. When her fingers touched him, awareness went through his body, and he shifted in his seat. "I'm glad Azadeh helped bring you home safely, and I don't want to put you or your family in danger."

"Let's take it one day at a time." He knew he should pull away from her touch, but it was hard. Instead he clasped her hand in his. "We'll figure this out. I promise."

"Okay..." Lynn's tongue ran across her lips quickly. "But at the first sign of danger for your family, I'm gone."

"Let's not worry about what we don't know yet. I'll see if Noah will watch Azadeh for a little bit, and I can take you around on the ATV."

"Okay." She smiled up at him.

He pulled his hands from hers and immediately missed her touch. Instead of reaching back for her hand, he cleared his throat. "Wait for a second. I'll get the door."

He jumped out of the truck and ran around the side before she had time to respond. Bryson opened the door and helped her climb down. They walked over to the barn in silence. His brother knelt on the ground with Azadeh next to him, a small black cat in her arms.

"Did you guys pick a name yet?"

"Yes, Ghost."

Bryson's throat tightened for a second. "Are you sure?"

Azadeh nodded and hugged the kitten closer to her body. "Yes, I take care of him, like you took care of me."

Lynn's eyes moved between him and Azadeh. He

knew she didn't understand what was going on. "Azadeh is naming her kitty after me." When she gave him a puzzled look, he added, "My call sign was Ghost."

"So was his nickname growing up." Noah snickered.

Bryson ignored his brother's comment. Lynn didn't need to hear the story about his childhood nickname, even though both of his brothers loved to tell it. "I'm going to show Lynn to her room and around the property. When we're done, we both need computers so we can look into her husband."

"Husband?" Noah asked.

"I thought we were divorced, but long story short, we aren't," Lynn grumbled.

"We'll watch Azadeh." Noah looked back at the house for a second. "Matilda and I will take Lynn's things in. Go have fun, and take her out by the mines. The snow shouldn't be too deep out there. Les was working in the mine this morning."

Bryson placed his hand on Lynn's back and directed her toward the ATV. He got on first, and she climbed on behind him, wrapping her hands around his waist. He realized too late that it might not be the best idea to have her wrapped around him. His body went on full alert when he felt her press against him. It took everything in him to hold back a groan.

For the next hour, they traveled around the countryside. He took her over to the gold mine to show her what the company Noah had hired was doing. He watched as she traced her fingers over the faint gold in the walls. His older brother's fiancée would be rich for years with the amount of gold in the mine. On the way out, he waved at the guard on duty and told him to keep an eye out for anything that looked out of the ordinary.

When he noticed Lynn shiver, he knew it was time to head back to the house. They climbed back on the ATV and barreled through the snow. Lynn giggled as white powder flew up around them. He'd had so much fun over the last hour, showing her around. It was easy to forget she was married.

He felt her hands tighten around his waist as they pulled back up to the barn and parked. Three men stood talking to Noah. Two he knew: Hank Patterson and Collin. The third man he didn't know personally, but Bryson recognized him and had a feeling that was why Lynn looked so grim.

"You don't have to talk to him."

"I know, but it's time I figure out why he didn't divorce me. It might explain why someone is trying to kill me."

Bryson put his hands in his pockets so he wouldn't reach out and grab Lynn's. They were going to talk to her husband.

CHAPTER 8

"Why didn't you sign the papers?" Lynn asked Gabriel. Hank, Collin, and Bryson sat with Lynn and Gabriel at the kitchen table. Matilda had taken Azadeh into another room. She didn't need to hear the conversation.

"Come on, Lynn. It's been three years. That's the only question you have?"

"Yes, I want to know why you didn't sign. Making some public video offering a reward to find me is ridiculous," Lynn ground out.

"Can we have this conversation in private?" Gabriel asked.

"No." Bryson didn't wait for Lynn to answer.

She smiled over at him before turning back to Gabriel. "Bryson is right. Whatever you have to say, you can say in front of these men. I have my reasons for not wanting to be alone with you. Now explain why you didn't sign the papers."

"We were friends for years before we got married. Why would you think I'd just sign the divorce papers? You're my wife."

Lynn tapped her fingernail on the wood table. "Well, you cheated on me. So you were already one leg out of the marriage."

"She was a mistake. We went out for dinner and had too much to drink and ended up together." Gabriel ran his hand through his hair.

Bryson wanted to reach across the table and strangle the man. He had on a polo and jeans. His hair was short. The man wasn't bad looking, but it didn't matter, he had treated Lynn like shit, and Bryson wanted the man gone.

"Stop making excuses," Lynn said. "When I got home, I looked through your computer. That wasn't the first time, and you asked her to dinner. Now tell me the real reason we aren't divorced."

"You went through my things?" Gabriel raised his voice.

"Yes," Lynn replied with no remorse. "Now explain the stupid reward for finding me and why you haven't signed the papers. My patience is wearing thin."

Gabriel eyed Lynn for a second before answering. "I needed to be married for five years to get my inheritance."

"You could've divorced me and started over."

"My mom loved you, and she wouldn't let me sign the papers. Hell, she was the one who made me do the broadcast."

Hank shook his head. "You knew where she was the whole time." It wasn't a question. It was a statement and the same one Bryson had on the tip of his tongue.

Gabriel shrugged. "Yes, last week was our five-year anniversary, and I can sign the papers now."

"There's something you aren't telling me." Lynn narrowed her eyes. "Why are you really here?"

"You really don't know?" Gabriel pinched the bridge of his nose. "I can't believe you signed the prenup without reading."

Lynn's cheeks turned pink from embarrassment. "I never expected to get divorced. Since I don't know what I missed, why don't you clue me in?"

"At five years, I get my inheritance and you get a ten-percent stake in my family company." Gabriel sighed. "You also get a seat on the board since I'm the oldest. My younger brothers aren't happy because you took their voting share at our five-year anniversary."

Bryson let out a low whistle. "That's a good enough reason to try to kill you."

"What are you talking about?" Gabriel asked. "I'm the only one who knew she was here. Over the past few years, I had a man checking to make sure she was okay. A month ago, when everything went down, I planned to come talk to you, but my dad had a heart attack, and I've taken over as CEO of the company."

"I don't want to be part of your company. I didn't marry you for the money," Lynn pointed out. "Let me just sign everything back to the family, and we can go our separate ways."

"It's not that easy," Gabriel insisted. "I need your help."

"Why would you expect me to help you?" Lynn leaned back in her chair and crossed her arms.

"We were friends for a long time, and I still consider you a close friend."

Lynn scrunched her brows. "You have a strange concept of close friends. We haven't talked in years."

"Close friend wasn't the correct words. Someone I can trust is more like it."

"What do you want me to do?" she asked.

"Keep your voting rights and a share of the company. I think someone on the board killed my father, and I'm not going to lose the only thing my father cared about."

"I won't agree to anything unless you sign the divorce papers."

Gabriel reached into his bag, pulled out a stack of papers, and slid them across the table. "I had my attorney draw up new papers with what you should get in the divorce. I know this is a lot to ask of you, but I need your help."

Lynn flipped through a few pages of the document. "I don't want your money."

"Five million dollars isn't much." Gabriel cleared his throat. "If you read farther on, in one year, you'll sign over your portion of the company to me for free."

"If we can fix the issue with your board member and settle things for you, would you allow Lynn to sign the company over to you sooner?" Bryson asked as he took the papers from Lynn's hand.

"Yes." He pinched the bridge of his nose. "My stepbrothers are fighting every aspect, but my father's will and Lynn's prenup are both ironclad. They can't do anything to change it."

Lynn clutched her hands together. "What happens if I'm killed?"

"Your shares go into holding until the board decides. If we were still married, they would go to me. Since we're signing divorce papers, the board would decide, and before you say you could make a will, it won't work. The bylaws are already in effect."

"So everyone on the board knows about this," Lynn said softly. "Wait, they think we're married, so it wouldn't matter."

"You're not the only one who's had a few close calls." Gabriel looked at Noah and Bryson for a few seconds. "Someone put a bomb on my plane before I came out here. Luckily the pilot did another inspection, or I would be dead. My share goes to the board as well to decide what to do with it."

Noah sat back in his chair. "What are your plans?"

"I'm going to head back to Seattle to figure out who on my board is corrupt. I owe it to my father to figure this out. I know it wasn't fair to you to not sign the papers."

Lynn shook her head. "We never loved each other. You wanted to make your dad happy, and I wanted a family."

"Do you have a security team you trust?" Noah asked as he typed away on his phone.

Gabriel shrugged. "I thought I did, but now I'm not so sure. The only person who knew about Lynn was my bodyguard. He was also the one who was supposed to check the plane but didn't show up when I was leaving."

"Hank, I know your men are pretty busy," Noah said. "I have a friend getting out of the CIA with contacts around the Seattle area. I think she would be a great bodyguard."

"Are you talking about Razor?" Hank let out a low whistle. "If you have a contact for her, go for it. I've wanted her on my team since I started the Brotherhood Protectors. She always told me she would retire when she got out."

"I can't have a woman protect me."

Noah turned and glared at Gabriel. "Razor would slice your throat if she ever heard you say shit like that. Some of the best soldiers I worked with were women. You need help, and she can do it. I've been texting with her for the last half hour. She agreed to help so we can figure out who is after both of you."

Lynn grabbed the pen off the table and signed the documents. "I signed. Noah has agreed to help you get out of this mess. Now sign the papers so I can start my life. I'm not trusting you to sign them when you leave. I want a signed copy to hold in case you don't take them to the courthouse."

"I know you guys didn't need to help." Gabriel reached over and scribbled his name across both copies. "Are you sure I'm not going to get your friend killed?"

"I wouldn't worry about her." Noah smiled. "Might recommend not making any more comments about her being a girl."

Lynn was excited she was about to be divorced. Once Gabriel submitted the documents to the courthouse, their marriage would be over. She still had to deal with him until the other part of her life was cleaned up. Bryson squeezed her leg under the table. His touch alone sent goose bumps through her body.

"Why are you helping me?" Gabriel asked the men around the table.

"We're helping Lynn."

"Thank you." Gabriel stood and walked around the side of the table. "I'm sorry for putting you through this. I know you didn't have to help, but I truly appreciate what you're doing."

Lynn leaned in and gave Gabriel a hug. "Take care. I don't have a phone yet. How will we stay in contact?"

"Don't worry about it." Noah shrugged. "I had his info the second you and Bryson told me he existed. I'll send him a text, and he can contact you through me."

Gabriel nodded before heading out the door.

"I'll fly back to Seattle with him to ensure he makes it safely," Collin said as he put on his jacket. "I've heard rumors about Razor. It would be nice to finally meet the legend."

Noah burst out laughing. "Not sure you'll feel the same after meeting her."

Hank hadn't said much during the meeting, but now he turned to Noah and smiled. "I know you have more contacts out in Seattle. You chose her because she'll be an ass to him."

"Maybe, but mostly she'll keep him alive. Give me an update when you get back from Seattle."

"Will do. Stay safe. We know someone is after Lynn, and we know why. We just don't know who it is."

Lynn gave Collin and Hank a hug before they walked out the door. Noah, Bryson, and Lynn walked into the living room. She sat down on the couch next to Azadeh. The young girl reached out and gripped her hand. Bryson took the seat on the other side of her.

Noah walked over and picked Matilda up then sat down and put her on his lap. The two were perfect for each other. Lynn had met Matilda's brother when she lived in Faith of the Glorious One. He was a great kid, and Matilda had done a good job of raising him.

Bryson didn't deserve to be put through her mess. She had money now. Maybe she could go on the run. A check was attached to the back of the divorce papers. Five million dollars. She didn't know what to do with the money. She didn't want it. Gabriel's money wasn't the reason she married him in the first place.

She settled into the couch and watched the news. Azadeh gripped her hand tighter when it went to world news and reported about a bombing in Jalalabad. When a man flashed across the screen, Bryson quickly turned the channel. Lynn was so wound up in her own problem, she had momentarily forgotten everything Azadeh had gone through.

Lynn didn't know what tomorrow would bring, but for tonight, she would hang out with the people helping her.

CHAPTER 9

Bryson leaned against the tack room door. Azadeh and Lynn stood outside Midnight's stall, filling his bucket with feed. It had taken a month for the judge to sign off on the divorce, but Gabriel had sent Noah the information today showing the divorce was final.

Bryson had just spoken with Gabriel over the phone and couldn't help but smile. Razor was putting him through the wringer. She was one hell of an agent. He had worked a few operations with her over the years. When someone became her friend, she would protect them for life, and she made sure their enemies never saw the light of day.

Gabriel had tried to tell her he was worried she would get hurt. It took everything in Bryson not to laugh when Gabriel told him she had flipped him on his back a second later and had her high heel pointed at the artery in his neck until he promised never to doubt her ability again.

Razor was working her way through Gabriel's company, looking for the person who had killed Gabriel's dad. It would be the same person who was after Lynn. Luckily nobody had come after them since Gabriel left. At night, Lynn and Bryson combed through the servers at RRT Consulting. Gabriel had given them full rights. Bryson loved to watch Lynn work. She'd written a program to help sort through the data.

Bryson had worked with a few programmers over the years. None were able to write a program so quickly with so much detail. During his time in the military, he had written a few scripts and small programs only to have them not work the first time he ran them. Most of the time it was because he didn't end a statement. Then he would have to comb through the code and figure out what he did wrong. Lynn's program worked the first time she ran it.

He waited a few minutes before he walked over to his girls. Bryson fell for Lynn each day a little more. They had talked about going on a date, but both wanted the divorce to be finalized first.

Lynn leaned down and whispered something in Azadeh's ear, and the young girl burst out laughing.

"What's so funny?" Bryson asked as he lifted Azadeh and tossed her into the air.

"Girl stuff, nothing you boys need to know

about." She winked at him before feeding a carrot to Midnight. "He's so much calmer." Midnight nudged Lynn's pocket, looking for another carrot.

"Hannah said he was abused. It takes time for an animal to trust again. The other day he threw his head back when Noah walked in." Bryson ran his hand along the horse's neck.

"It's okay, Midnight. Noah is scary sometimes," she whispered to the horse.

Bryson wanted to ask what she planned to do after they made sure the man after her was gone. *Would she stay in Montana or go back to Seattle?* He reached up and scratched behind Midnight's ear. *How would the horse take it when she left, or would she take him with her and leave me with nothing to remember her by?* He wasn't ready to ask his questions because he was worried what her response might be. Deep down he knew she would be perfect for him and Azadeh, but maybe it would be too much to ask for her to help raise Azadeh.

"Bryson?"

"Yes?" He turned toward Azadeh.

"Are we moving somewhere else?" she asked.

He frowned down at her. "I know it's not the same as where you grew up, but I have you registered to start school in January. Do you not like living here?"

"I like it here. Lynn said she was leaving."

Lynn blushed. "Not right away." Lynn knelt down

so she was eye level with Azadeh. "I can't stay here forever. Once the bad guy is in jail, I'm going to have to find a place to live."

"I don't want you to leave us," Azadeh whispered. A small tear escaped the young girl's eye, and it almost broke Bryson's heart. Lynn was already talking about leaving, and it affected Azadeh as much as it did him. He was just able to hide his emotions a little better than the young girl.

"You don't have to worry about finding a place. Montana Gold will always have room for you." He reached out and gripped her hand.

Whatever he said had upset her.

Lynn reached up and wiped her eye. "You mean that?" She looked into his eyes, searching for something he didn't understand. "This is the second time in my life I feel like I have a place to call home. I know I'm not part of your family, but it's starting to feel like I have a place here."

The barn and animals around him disappeared as he looked down at her. A light sheen still covered her eyes, but they weren't tears of sadness. He searched his brain for the right words, but the only ones that came to mind would sound so caveman-like, and he didn't want to wreck the moment.

Bryson pulled Lynn into his arms. "I don't know about you, but I don't have these feelings about family." He dipped his head, and his lips brushed across hers for a second. Aware of Azadeh being close, he didn't want to lose control in front of her. "I've waited over a month to taste those lips."

"Wow." She ran her fingers across them. "You're right, the feelings I have for you aren't something you should have for a family member."

Bryson stepped back for a second. "Azadeh, can you go into the house and see if Matilda needs help?"

The young girl stared up at him for a second before turning and running toward the house. She barely cleared the barn before Bryson wrapped his arms around Lynn, his mouth capturing her lips. His tongue pushed past them to sweep across her tongue. The kiss wasn't sweet like when Azadeh was near. This kiss was claiming her as his. He needed her as much as he needed his next breath. For the past four weeks, he had waited to do just that.

He pulled back and rested his forehead against hers. "I've wanted to do that since the first time I saw you."

Lynn's lips ticked upward. "I've waited just as long. From the way you just kissed me, I assume you talked to Gabriel."

Bryson had wanted to wait a little longer before he took her in his arms, but when she'd looked up at him earlier in the barn, it was all he could do to hold back. "Yes, Gabriel called before I came out here. He also sent a copy of the papers signed by the judge."

She smiled. "I'm officially divorced. Most people

would be sad, but I'm excited for the next step in my life."

"Have you thought about your next step much?" Bryson needed her in his arms. He reached out and pulled her close.

Lynn rested her head on his chest. The two of them fit perfectly together, and he loved having her in his arms.

Bryson had spent his early years sleeping with whoever he could pick up from the bar each night. About five years ago that got old, and he didn't want meaningless sex. As much as he tried, it wasn't easy to find someone who wanted to be with him. He was gone more than he was home. And now he had to think about Azadeh as well. *Would Lynn want to be a part of Azadeh's life?*

"I mentioned to Midnight that I had no clue how I would leave him or you. That's what Azadeh must have heard. We barely know each other. Is it strange that I don't want to leave you when this is all over?"

"I don't want you to leave." He kissed the top of her nose. "You realize that if you do stay and we try to date, Azadeh will always be a part of my life. I won't leave her."

Lynn stepped out of his arms and glared at him. "What made you think I wouldn't want to be part of Azadeh's life? That little girl has wormed her way into my heart."

Bryson didn't like that she was so far away. The

second she stepped out of his arms, he missed her and her touch. Stepping forward, he tugged her back into his arms. When she rubbed against him, his other body part got excited. He took a couple of deep breaths, trying to get his body back under control. She had just admitted to wanting to get to know him better. He didn't want her to feel pressure, even though his dick had been hard since the day he'd pulled her out of the truck.

He leaned forward and gently pressed his lips to hers one more time before stepping back. "I think it's almost time for dinner."

She smiled up at him. "I know something else I would rather have."

"You can't say things like that. I'm trying to be a gentleman and get to know you better." He pulled her in tighter. "Let me take you out on a date first."

"I like that. Should we have Azadeh come with us?"

"She can come with us next time."

Lynn stood on her tippy-toes and kissed his lips before turning toward the house. He watched as her ass swayed in her tight jeans. Knowing she was available, he couldn't wait to get a taste of her.

~

LYNN ADDED an extra sway to her step as she walked

out of the barn and couldn't help but grin when she heard Bryson groan.

Forty-six days she waited for that kiss. Bryson was an honorable man. Even though he knew she was going through the divorce process, he wouldn't touch her until it was final. She didn't know how he was able to act so unaffected. It took everything in her not to sit and stare when he worked on the ranch.

Every second she spent with him and Azadeh made her feel like she had finally found what she was looking for. It wasn't a place. It was the people. Even Noah and Matilda had made her feel like she was family. She only worried Bryson might change his mind. She had fallen for him so much in the past few weeks, she didn't know what she would do if he decided he didn't have time for a girlfriend.

She could only take it one day at a time. Bryson was worth losing her heart for. Azadeh and the sexy cowboy had already taken part of her heart. She hoped that once they found the man after her, Bryson would feel the same way.

Lynn walked into the kitchen and grabbed a Coke out of the fridge. Matilda was cutting up a tomato on the cutting board. She was making a salad to go along with the roast in the oven. The house smelled amazing. Keith had kept them on a strict diet for the last three years. Lynn had missed having home-cooked meals instead of microwaved ones.

"Did Bryson tell you the good news?" Matilda asked with a smile.

Lynn reached over and grabbed a tomato slice off the board and popped it into her mouth. "Yes. How did you find out?"

"Noah overheard the conversation." Matilda grabbed an onion next and started to dice it. "So are you going to finally kiss, or are we going to keep dancing around your feelings?"

Lynn could feel her cheeks burning.

"Damn, that was quick. He must've gotten the call and rushed outside to see you."

"Maybe."

"He did." Matlida pointed at her. "It's written all over your face. Was it everything you wanted?"

"The kiss was amazing. Hell, I wanted more, but he wants to get to know me better."

"If you want to do something tomorrow night, we can take Azadeh into Bozeman for a movie and watch her the following morning."

"That would be so cool, but don't feel like you have to watch her for us. It's been so nice the last few days that we could have a picnic or something outside."

"It's not a problem, and I know Noah loves to spend time with her. Maybe Sebastian can meet us at the movies when we're in town. I don't like going very long without talking to him."

Lynn popped another tomato into her mouth. "I

love your brother. Make sure to tell him hello from me if he meets you tomorrow." Regret filled her about how they'd met. "I don't know if I've said it to you before, but I'm sorry for what your brother went through."

"Everything happens for a reason. If he hadn't joined the crazy cult and given away all my money, I would never have met Noah." Matilda paused for a second. "I went through hell for three months, and I wouldn't go back and change a thing. Life is a long chain of events. If you hadn't found your husband cheating, you never would've joined Faith of the Glorious One, and you never would've met Bryson. The best thing you can do is take one day at a time," Matilda suggested.

"You're right, I need to stop dwelling on the things I can't change and focus on what I can do to help others."

"See, now you're talking. Life is too short to live in your past. Now, what do you plan to do with Bryson tomorrow besides sex?"

Lynn laughed. "I'm not even sure sex is going to happen. He insists on going slow. Like we haven't tiptoed around our attraction since we met."

"I see the way he looks at you." Matilda chopped the lettuce up quickly and threw it in the bowl. "You put something sexy on, and that man won't be able to keep his hands off you."

"I'm not sure what he has planned, but I'm going

to make sure it ends with him in my bed or me in his."

"Did he say if Razor was able to find out who's after you?"

Lynn felt the tension in her shoulders tightened. "No, she hasn't found anything. All board members are clean from what she can find, but she's going to keep looking."

"They will find the person."

"Once they find out who's after me, I can move back to Brighter Days or find a place in town."

Matilda narrowed her eyes. "This place is big enough for all of us. I don't expect you to move out. We like having you here."

"I like being here, but your relationship is still so new. Now you've added a few more people to the house."

"Growing up, it was just Sebastian and me." Matilda shrugged. "Having Noah's brother and you near makes me happy. It would be even better if Grayson would come up here and build another house on the land."

"From the way Bryson talks, it would take a lot for Kara to come live up here again."

Lynn didn't blame Kara for not wanting to live on the land. She had too many bad memories of her dad and sad memories of her mom dying.

Bryson, Noah, and Azadeh came into the kitchen and gathered around the dining room table. Lynn loved how, each night, they all ate together. They would talk about what was going on in the small town of Eagle Ridge, and Noah would tell embarrassing stories about Bryson. Then Bryson would get his brother back with embarrassing stories of his own.

Each night, they took turns doing the dishes. Tonight was Noah and Matilda's turn. While the couple worked on the dishes, Lynn went and watched a cartoon with Azadeh and Bryson. Azadeh loved watching Bugs Bunny. By the time the credits rolled, the little girl could no longer keep her eyes open. Bryson picked sleeping Azadeh up from the couch and carried her to her room.

When Lynn exited the bathroom after brushing her teeth, Bryson was on the other side waiting for her. He smiled down at her before pulling her into his arms and pressing his lips against hers. She wrapped her arms around his neck and pulled him in closer. He pulled away too soon. She wanted more.

"Go to sleep, and tomorrow we'll go on a date."

Lynn didn't know how on earth she would fall asleep after he woke her body up with that kiss. Her insides heated just from being in his arms. He stopped outside her bedroom and placed one more gentle kiss on her lips before turning and going into the room across the hall.

She let out a frustrated breath before changing into her T-shirt and shorts. When she climbed into bed, all she could think about was the kiss from the man across the hall. *Is he lying in bed thinking about the same thing?* She reached up and touched her lips, and they still tingled from his kiss.

Tomorrow would be her first date with Bryson, and she couldn't wait to find out what they were going to do. She closed her eyes and tried to think about anything other than Bryson or she would never fall asleep.

CHAPTER 10

BRYSON'S ALARM sounded too early. He hadn't slept well throughout the night. His thoughts turned to Lynn every time he closed his eyes. A few times over, he stopped himself from getting out of bed and knocking on her door. He wondered if she was asleep or thinking about him as much as he was about her.

Would she want to stay in Eagle Ridge? How does she feel about having kids? She had mentioned a few times that she missed writing code. *Would living on a ranch be enough for her?*

The longer he laid in bed, the more his mind wandered to questions he couldn't answer, and if he thought about her beautiful body, his mind went straight to sex.

Bryson could hear the laughter coming from downstairs. He rose from bed and grabbed a pair of shorts from the floor. He thought about Lynn's body for a second, and he was hard. A cold shower called his name before he went downstairs. It was the only thing that could get his body back under control.

He needed to start thinking about what would happen next. Kara's house was a good size, but he didn't want to stay under the same roof as his brother and Matilda. The way Noah looked at Matilda, it was only a matter of time before he asked her to marry him. The newlyweds wouldn't want them underfoot. But moving would be hard with Azadeh starting school in a few weeks.

Tonight he would broach the subject of what Lynn wanted to do and where she would love to live.

With each day that passed, he felt the connection growing between him and Lynn. He loved to sit back and watch her play with Azadeh. He knew he wasn't the only one attached to Lynn. Azadeh sat next to her any second she could. Azadeh was also like a little sponge, taking in any information Lynn told her.

Bozeman wasn't too far away, and he planned to take Lynn out for a nice dinner. Noah had agreed to watch Azadeh for the day and night. Since her rescue, Lynn hadn't left Eagle Ridge. He figured a night out on the town would be fun for them both.

He grabbed a pair of jeans and a long-sleeved shirt before heading into the bathroom. His shower was quick and cold. Hopefully he would be able to keep his body in line for the remainder of the day.

Bryson went down the old staircase toward the

kitchen. The sound of Azadeh giggling brought a smile to his face. When he rounded the corner, she was doing a silly dance at the head of the table.

Noah stood at the stove, one arm wrapped around Matilda, the other flipping pancakes.

Lynn sat at the table, sipping a cup of coffee. When she heard his footsteps, she turned, and her pretty blue eyes landed on him. She gave him a welcoming smile before pulling out the chair next to her. "Come join us. Azadeh was showing us a dance she learned from a YouTube video." She pushed Azadeh's tablet toward him and whispered, "We might need to look at parental controls for what she watches. She's trying to mimic a rap video she found."

"I never thought about parental controls." Bryson logged into YouTube on the iPad and quickly changed the settings. "Fixed." He sighed. "I really should've done that before I gave it to her."

Lynn touched his forearm, and awareness went through his body. The cold shower did nothing to help with his desire to be with her.

"I wouldn't have thought of it either," Lynn said. "But kids seem to figure out technology faster than adults, even ones who use technology every day."

"I agree." Noah walked over and set a stack of pancakes on the table. It was enough to feed an army. "The younger guys becoming agents always have the tech figured out within seconds."

Bryson nodded, understanding what his brother was talking about when it came to the younger generation. Each recruit in his unit would come in eager to add their knowledge to help. Bryson would miss working alongside his brothers, but it was time to start a new chapter in his life. One thing he knew for sure was he wanted Lynn to be part of that life going forward. She looked up at him and smiled before putting a pancake and bacon on Azadeh's plate. The young girl could eat as much as him some days, and she dug into the fluffy pancake before taking a sip of her milk.

Matilda walked over to the table and handed him a cup of black coffee, just the way he liked it. Coffee was the perfect thing to go with the cold Montana morning.

"Thank you!"

"I still don't know how you drink it like that." Lynn smiled before taking a sip of her coffee filled with sugar and milk.

"Some places where I was stationed didn't have access to all the things you like in your coffee," Bryson said. "It was easier to drink it black if I had it at all."

"Right there is the reason I stopped drinking coffee. Most of the time, it tasted closer to motor oil than coffee." Noah shook his head before taking a gulp of his orange juice.

Azadeh popped the last piece of pancake into her

mouth. "More, please."

Lynn reached over and gave her another one. It wasn't long before Noah was telling a story about his time in the military and Azadeh was laughing at something he'd done.

Noah rested his elbows on the table. "Azadeh, do you think you could spend a day away from your cat and come with Matilda and me? We wanted to do some Christmas shopping."

"Yes." Then she reached out and grabbed Lynn's hand. "You come with too."

Bryson didn't wait for Lynn to reply. "Not today, Azadeh. Lynn and I are going to do some of our own shopping. We can't get you a gift when you're along."

"I don't need anything. I like living here enough."

He hated how she always felt she was a burden to him. Over time, he knew she would start to feel like part of the family and not someone he had saved who now owed him.

"Do you mind taking Azadeh over to Brighter Days for a little while?" Bryson took a bite of his bacon before continuing. "I heard Hannah will be working with the horses today."

"I think that's a great idea," Matilda said. "I made a painting for Hannah the other day and need to give it to her."

Matilda was an amazing landscape artist. She had opened a store online, and her pictures sold as quickly as she put them up. Two weeks ago, she'd made one of Azadeh sitting in the barn, cradling her kitten to her chest. Bryson put the picture up in the room where he was staying.

The main reason he wanted them to stop by Brighter Days was for Hannah to talk with Azadeh for a little while. He knew he should find her a counselor in Bozeman, and he planned to in the near future. First, he had to make sure nobody was after her.

He checked the links online. Her uncle had sent out a reward, but Bryson didn't think her uncle would try anything on US soil.

"What are your plans for the day?" Noah asked.

Bryson grabbed another pancake. "It's supposed to be in the upper fifties. The weather's been crazy this winter. It doesn't feel like Christmas is only two weeks away. I figured we would take the horses out and go for a nice picnic and later drive into Bozeman to catch a movie."

"I can't wait to ride Midnight."

"I'm not sure he's ready. Why don't we take the other two?"

Lynn narrowed her eyes at him. "Midnight will do just fine." She got up from the table and took her plate to the sink. "I'm going to go talk with him right now."

Noah coughed to cover up his laugh. "Let me know if he talks back."

"He will." She smiled before heading out the door.

"Lynn can talk to horses?"

"No, Azadeh." Bryson let out a groan. "She was joking."

The young girl frowned. "But she told me the other day the horse likes carrots."

"All horses like carrots." Bryson got up from the table and took his and Azadeh's plates to the sink. "Let's go out to the barn and help her get ready."

Azadeh jumped up to grab her jacket. "I'm going to go check on Ghost!" she yelled before running out the door.

Noah crossed his arms. "She is going to be a handful."

"I know." Bryson slipped on his light jacket. "But I wouldn't change what happened. Well, it would've been nice not to have been stuck in a cell for days."

"Have you heard anything about Ricky?"

"They're still looking for him. They've found no sign he left the Middle East," Bryson told his brother. He had communicated back and forth with his commander. Carson had worked to find as much information as he could on Ricky. With what Bryson had given him, they'd taken down a small drug ring.

"Something doesn't feel right." Noah ran his hand through his hair. "With the intel you gave, they took down his operation? I'm surprised he hasn't come after you."

"Lynn helped me create a program that's running all the scanned passports coming into the US. She also programmed an alert into the system. We can't spend our days hiding, thinking he might attack."

"You're right."

Matilda walked over and handed him a bag. When he looked inside, it had a couple of sandwiches and a bag of chips.

"I figured you guys might get hungry on the ride. It's so nice out that you can sit and have a meal up by the cave."

He nodded. "Thank you. If Azadeh needs me for anything today, please call."

"Don't worry about it. Noah and I can handle a little girl. It will be fun to take her to the mall. Noah's always in such a hurry to leave. Now Azadeh and I can look at all the pretty things."

"Thank you." Bryson walked outside, carrying the bag of food. Azadeh was sitting on the ground in front of the barn with her black kitten in her arms. Lynn led two horses out of the barn, Midnight and Whiskey. Midnight pranced next to her and threw his head up a few times. Whiskey walked along without a care in the world.

"Are you sure I can't talk you into riding Whiskey?"

Lynn glared at him before running her hand along Midnight's neck. "I'll be fine."

Bryson grabbed Whiskey's reins out of her hands. "I want to go on record and say I think this is a bad idea."

"Stop putting negative thoughts into the universe." She slipped her foot into the stirrup and pulled herself up. "Look, he's doing just fine."

Midnight pranced a little. Lynn quickly spun him in a circle, and he calmed down. Knowing she wasn't going to change her mind, Bryson got on Whiskey. The old horse didn't move until he squeezed his legs.

Lynn trotted next to him as they went down the trail to the back of the land. Every so often, Bryson would catch Lynn looking toward the north property line. They couldn't see the house to the north, but he knew what was there.

"Does it bother you, living this close?"

She didn't answer right away. "No. I wish I would've done something sooner, but when I figured it out, it wasn't what I thought it would be. Keith wouldn't let me leave, and then I stopped trying."

They spent the next half hour talking about what it was like living in the cult. He couldn't imagine what it would be like to be trapped inside for three years. After a few days inside when it got cold out, Bryson would go stir-crazy.

Lynn was right about Midnight being ready for a ride. In the beginning, he was antsy, but as the walk progressed, he calmed down and walked next to Whiskey.

They stopped in front of the entrance to the mine. Bryson quickly jumped off Whiskey and came to Midnight's side to help Lynn down. She didn't protest when he grabbed her around the waist and pulled her down. Her arms went around his shoulders, and she pressed her soft lips to his. The kiss was gentle at first until he pulled her in tighter.

Bryson pulled a blanket out of his saddlebag and spread it across the ground. The warm sun beat down, and he stripped off his jacket. Lynn sat next to him, and he pulled her into his arms.

"I know you didn't have a normal childhood, but did you love something about Christmas?"

Lynn rested her head on his shoulder. "Ms. Jackson made Christmas fun, but I never felt like part of her family. It wasn't because she didn't try. She had three biological kids of her own, and they only came around during holidays, so she spent much of the day talking with them. I just want to spend Christmas with the people I enjoy being around."

"Who's that?" Bryson joked.

Lynn playfully nudged him. "You and Azadeh, silly. How about you? What's your favorite thing about Christmas?"

"Before my mom passed, she would have all three boys help cook Christmas dinner. We had so much fun cooking and joking with each other. My dad was always in charge of the turkey, and we made everything else."

"You guys were close."

"Yes, and then it was hard when Grayson left for the Navy, and Noah left the following year. Then it was just Dad and me. After Mom died, Dad wasn't the same, and Grayson and Noah never came back."

"Is Grayson going to come up here for Christmas this year? I would love to meet him."

"I think he will. Are you getting hungry?" Bryson reached into his bag and pulled out the food.

Lynn grabbed one of the sandwiches. "Yes, thank you."

"We should take Azadeh to pick out a Christmas tree."

Lynn took a bite of her sandwich. "I've never done that be—" Her words were cut off when the sound of a shot rang out.

"What the fuck?" Bryson grunted as he rolled Lynn to the side behind a rock.

It didn't stop the shooter. Bullets flew past, a few hitting the rock they crouched behind. Bryson cursed himself for leaving his gun in the saddlebags. He wouldn't be able to get to them now since the horses had taken off running when the first shot was fired.

"Do you think it's the same person who's after Gabriel?"

"I'm not sure." Bryson sighed. "But it looks like we're going to be here awhile. Let's get into the mine and see if one of the workers left something for us to protect ourselves with."

He hoped going into the mine was the right decision.

CHAPTER 11

Lynn was terrified. The day the truck she was driving had its breaks cut had been petrifying, but that was nothing compared to having shots fired at her. Another one hit the front of the rock. Whoever was shooting hadn't stopped or slowed down, even though Lynn and Bryson were behind the rock. When the horses had taken off running, her heart had stopped.

Bryson slowly moved to the side, raised his hand, and lowered it quickly. Another round of shots fired.

"At least it's only one shooter."

Lynn huffed, "Really, only one. I don't see how one is okay."

"It could have been a few," Bryson said. "One I might be able to handle." His frown deepened. "We need to get you out of sight so I can figure out how to stop this man."

Lynn tried to peek around the large rock, but Bryson pulled her against him. "Maybe the guy will just leave."

"Whoever's out there was waiting for you. But they aren't professionally trained."

"They're good enough. We didn't see them." She tugged her arm out of Bryson's grip. "What makes you think they aren't trained?"

"A trained marksman would've hit the target. I counted at least eight rounds, and he didn't come near us."

Lynn didn't know how Bryson had taken the time to count the rounds. Her only thought was to get to safety when the second shot rang out. The first shot hadn't registered until Bryson was tugging her behind the large rock. If they wanted to hide in the mine, they would need to step out from behind the rock for a few steps.

"What's the plan?" Lynn whispered.

"I need to get you into the mine, and then I can try to take down the person after us." Bryson ran his hand through his hair for the tenth time. She noticed he did it every time he was stressed, and their current situation was definitely stressful.

Lynn heard an engine start in the distance.

Bryson put a finger to his lips for a second. "I think the person left."

When she went to stand, Bryson pulled her back down. "I said I think. You aren't going to be the person to test my theory. Wait here." Bryson stood up. They heard nothing. He crouched back down near her. Everything they needed was on the horses. That included the cell phone she normally kept tucked in her pocket but had been scared would fall out during the ride.

Bryson offered her his hand, and she stood next to him. Instead of leading her back down the trail, he led her into the mine.

Lynn took in the cave-like space. "Why aren't we heading back to the house?"

"We would be left exposed. We're going to have to wait until dark so we can sneak back. I heard someone drive off, but I'm not sure how far they went or if they did that to see if they could get us to come out of hiding."

"I haven't been this far in the mine before." She ran her fingers along the wall. Lanterns illuminated the walkway. "I can't believe how much gold is down here."

"Now I wish I hadn't told the guards to take the morning off and come back later."

"Nothing we can do about it now unless you brought your phone." Lynn made a mental note to always carry her phone on her person.

"Nope, mine's on the horse along with my gun. Looks like we're going to be here for a while."

"Well, should we sit here and get to know each other better?"

"How do you feel about swimming?"

She glanced around the cave. It wasn't cold inside, but it wasn't warm, and she couldn't imagine the water would be warm either. "I think it's a little cold to swim."

"Noah showed me where there's a natural hot spring down here. He said he's taken Matilda down here a couple of times. Do you want to see if we can find it?"

"Sure." She didn't have any better plans.

Bryson twined his fingers with hers. "Should be around this last turn."

"How pretty." Like much of Montana, the natural earth was breathtaking. She loved seeing the sunrise over the mountains and the leaves turn in the fall. At times, she missed the rush of the city, but the beauty of the country outweighed everything she missed.

"The shimmer on the walls is small amounts of sunlight reflecting off the gold." Bryson ran his fingers along a vein in the wall. "Kara decided she never wanted this section of the mine touched and wanted to preserve it. Her trust and the gold they're pulling out will be enough to support six generations."

"Did she quit her job?"

"Nope. She works in the ER." Bryson bent down, pulled off his cowboy boots, and set them to the side. Next he went to work unbuttoning his shirt.

Lynn covered her eyes with her hand. "Why are you stripping?"

"I don't want to get my clothes wet when I go into the spring." He motioned to the large pond in the middle of the cave opening. Steam rolled off the top.

Lynn eyed the water for a second. She couldn't see how deep it was or if something was in there. It was too dark to tell. She worried some creature might come and bite a part of her body she didn't want to share with nature. "Have you gone in there before?"

Bryson walked past her, naked. She couldn't help but stare at his tight ass as it flexed with each step toward the water. He said something, but her mind was so lost watching his every muscle move, she hadn't caught what he said.

She cleared her throat. "I'm sorry. What did you say?"

Bryson sank into the water before turning. His lips twitched up. "Did you like the view?"

"I don't know what you're talking about." She wasn't going to let him have all the fun. She grabbed the bottom of her shirt and pulled it over her head. Leaning down, she quickly removed her shoes and jeans next. She stood in the middle of the mine in her bra and panties, and it was cold. "Is the water cold?"

"Come in and find out." Bryson's voice was husky.

She dipped her toes in the water, and it was warm. It felt like a lukewarm bath. She walked into the water until it was up to her waist. She reached behind her back and slowly removed her bra.

Bryson was next to her within seconds, and his strong arms wrapped around her. "You are the sexiest woman I've ever seen," he whispered into her ear.

"You're not too bad yourself," she said before pressing her lips to his.

He cupped her butt with both hands, and she wrapped her legs around him. The water splashed around them, and the only thing she cared about was Bryson. Not the person who shot at them. Not her ex-husband, and not the million things going on in the world.

Lynn ran her hands through Bryson's hair and deepened the kiss. Her breasts pressed against his chest. No matter how much she tried to pull him closer, she couldn't get close enough.

Bryson slowly pulled them over to the edge of the water and sat down. She straddled his legs and captured his lips. Goose bumps rose on her flesh where his fingers ran down the small of her back before he cupped her ass.

His erection pushed against her belly, demonstrating he was as aroused as she.

After weeks of tiptoeing around their affection, she was ready to combust. If the kiss was anything to go by, she knew they were compatible and couldn't wait to be together.

"When I asked you to come out here today, this wasn't my plan."

She smiled against his lips before pulling back. "You mean you didn't plant a guy to take shots at us so I would hide with you inside a mine until it got dark so we could walk back?"

"Smart-ass." Bryson sighed. "No, I didn't think this through. I don't have protection with me."

Lynn leaned back and ran her fingers down his chest. "I have an IUD, and when I was rescued, I had a full panel of tests. I'm clean."

Bryson reached up and combed a strand of hair behind her ear. "I was tested a few months ago, and I haven't been with anyone since." He leaned forward and ran kisses up her neck until he was right next to her ear. "I don't want to rush you."

Rush, she felt like they'd been taking their sweet time. The sexual tension had increased each day, and she didn't want to wait any longer. She had no clue what tomorrow would bring, but she was willing to see where this led.

Lynn leaned forward and captured his lips. She reached between them and poised herself above his hard cock. "I want you," she whispered into his mouth as she slowly lowered herself, taking every inch of his length into her. When he was fully in her, he grabbed her hips to stop her from moving.

"You feel so good," he said. "Why did we wait this long?"

"Bryson," she whined, wanting him to move his hands so she could move.

"You want something?" he asked before capturing her nipple between his lips. He relaxed his hands on her hips but didn't remove them. "Slow," he said around her nipple.

"I need you." She arched her back, pushing her boob farther into Bryson's mouth. "I love your lips on me."

"Like this?" He took the other nipple in his mouth and grasped her first nipple with his free hand. Everything faded around them. It was just Bryson and her. Nothing else. She had never experienced lovemaking on such an intimate level.

Bryson shifted them into the water so he was able to leverage himself better. She felt herself getting close to the edge. Lynn wrapped her arms around Bryson, clinging to him as he thrust into her.

She felt her climax approaching, and she couldn't hold on any longer as Bryson buried himself deep inside her. He went over the edge at the same time, calling out her name.

Laughter bubbled up in her throat as her name echoed through the cave. "I feel like you announced to the world that you claimed me."

Bryson breathed heavily as he rested his forehead against Lynn's. "I hope the world heard me. I want everyone to know we're together."

"I like that." She smiled as he slowly pulled out of her.

He sat down on a rock in the water and positioned her on his lap. "Next time, it will be in a bed so I can spend hours worshipping you."

Her body still felt weak from the lovemaking. She didn't know how she would last for hours. "That was amazing."

"Yes," he said. "But you deserved better."

She rested an arm around his neck. "It was perfect, and I can't wait to do it again."

Bryson's body tensed at the sound of footsteps walking down the path. "Get behind me." He quickly pushed her behind him as a light flashed into the open room.

She watched as three large men walked through the entrance. It was too dark to make out their faces. She hoped they were the good guys and not who had shot at them a little while ago.

CHAPTER 12

"Turn around," Bryson growled. He knew who the three men were the second his eyes landed on them.

It was too dark in the mine to see Noah's facial expression. If he had to guess, his brother rolled his eyes.

"Really, you got shot at, and instead of figuring out who it was, you went swimming."

Well, if his brother wasn't going to turn around, he would get an eyeful. Bryson slowly walked out of the water, paying no attention to the three men. Taz and Collin quickly turned as Bryson got out. "I didn't have a gun or a phone. No way was I going to leave Lynn by herself. Then I remembered you talking about this great spring."

"It is nice," Noah replied.

Lynn cleared her throat behind him. "Can we stop talking until we're all dressed?"

Bryson quickly put on his boxers and jeans, leaving his shirt off until Lynn was dressed. Noah turned around while she quickly put her clothes back on. Bryson wished they'd had more time together before his brother showed up.

"I planned to walk back once the sun went down. I wasn't sure where the shooter was, so I didn't want to put Lynn in danger."

Noah nodded. "The shooter had a long-range rifle. He was over at the Faith of the Glorious One."

Lynn gasped next to Bryson. "I thought the property was taken over by the feds. How is someone there again?"

Noah rolled his neck. "The feds have taken it over." He wrinkled his brow. "But they aren't out there anymore. They don't even have a patrol around the area." Noah took a few steps toward them and wrapped his brother in a hug. "I was worried when Fedrick called and said he heard shots fired."

"Fedrick?" Bryson asked.

"He's one of the guards for the mine. They were still patrolling, just not close enough for you to see."

"If they heard shots, why did it take so long for you to get here?" On the inside, he was glad it took his brother a while. It wouldn't have bothered him if Noah had shown up a half hour earlier, but he knew Lynn would've been embarrassed, and he didn't want her to feel that way around his brother.

Noah patted Bryson on the back. "We did our job

and went and got the bad guy. Would you have preferred we come here and let the man go?"

"Who was it?" Lynn asked. The same question was on the tip of Bryson's tongue.

"It was Gabriel's two brothers," Noah replied. He turned and walked toward the exit of the mine.

Bryson reached down and grabbed Lynn's hand as they walked out. He had a sudden urge to get back to Azadeh. He knew he had no rational reason to make sure she was okay. Luckily she wasn't anywhere near the shooting. In addition, since Noah knew about a shooter, he would've made sure someone was with Matilda and Azadeh.

"Why?" Lynn asked as she shielded her eyes from the bright sun. "As far as they knew, if I die before Gabriel, it goes to Gabriel."

Collin frowned. "That is what Gabriel said, but the men we have in custody are singing a different song. We called Razor after we spoke to the people who shot at you. She found no evidence that Gabriel's life was ever in danger."

"None of this makes sense."

"It will." Taz handed them a couple of bottles of water from the ATV. "Gabriel showed us a prenup that wasn't real. Razor was able to get her hands on the real one. He used the fact that you never read it to his advantage."

Bryson pulled Lynn close, waiting for someone to finish telling him the story. He hated that Gabriel had taken advantage of Lynn and was the reason someone was trying to kill her. With each passing minute, the more he wanted to fly to Seattle and strangle the man.

"The part about you being married for five years for him to get his inheritance is correct. Also, the part where you get ten percent of the company. We think he knew all along that you never read the prenup, and when you joined Faith of the Glorious One, he used it to his advantage."

Lynn's shoulders slumped. "He was standing with me when I signed the document. You're right. He knew from the beginning that I never read it. Hell, Gabriel was the one who insisted everything in it was what we had discussed. The only thing we discussed was that if we divorced, I would get five million dollars and nothing else."

"Gabriel's dad is highly against divorce. When you hit your five-year anniversary, Gabriel got his share of the inheritance plus his share of the company, but the prenup says that if you get divorced, you still keep your share and your voting rights. The bylaws state that you can't turn the shares over to Gabriel."

"What happens if I die?" she asked.

Noah ran his hand through his hair and let out a frustrated breath. "That's when he gets them back. With his father dead, nobody can change the fact that he will have sixty percent of the company and can do what he wants."

Bryson clenched his fist. "Was Razor able to take him in?"

"The problem is that the men here insist they did it on their own. Which we now know is a lie. If we had to guess, we think Gabriel had them kill his dad as well."

So everything was an act to get controlling shares of his company. They needed to figure out a way to get rid of the shares. "Can she sell the shares to someone else?"

"Yes, and I already made that call for you. What better way to get rid of the shares than to sell them to a mercenary company?" Noah smirked.

Lynn looked up at him. "Who?"

"I assume he called the Ross brothers." Bryson glanced over at Noah resting his foot against the ATV with a smug smile on his face. "And from the look on your face, I'm guessing they're excited to own ten percent of the company." Antonio and Asher had already done so much for him. He didn't know how he would ever repay their family. He knew if they hadn't been in Jalalabad at the right time, he wouldn't have been standing there, having that conversation.

The sound of an ATV caught Bryson's attention, and he turned to the south to see Matilda driving. A little head poked out from her side, watching the trail. Bryson couldn't help but smile as he saw Azadeh coming down the trail.

Matilda had barely pulled to a stop before Azadeh

jumped off and ran toward him full force. His heart melted when she threw her arms around his waist and held him close for a second before turning and doing the same to Lynn. "I wanted to help."

Bryson grabbed her under her armpits and picked her up. "You need to stay safe. If you're in danger, you hide. I don't want anything to happen to you."

Lynn turned toward his brother. "So is it over, or will he keep coming for me?"

"Antonio is working on the sale of the shares for you. By the end of the day, you will be richer, and Gabriel will have no reason to come after you. You'll need to sign a few things tonight, but for the most part, you're out of danger."

"Well then, dinner is on me tonight."

~

Lynn's cheeks hurt from smiling so much. She was so excited everyone wanted to celebrate with her. Once they returned to the house and showered, everyone piled into the SUVs and headed to Bozeman for dinner. Taz and Hannah were in the SUV behind them.

It felt like a weight had been lifted, and she no longer had to look over her shoulder every second. She also had more money than she knew what to do with. Now she had to decide what she wanted to do next. Bryson reached over and gripped her hand, and she knew that whatever her plans were, they would include him.

"Now that you're rich, what do you plan to do next?" Hannah asked her.

Lynn shrugged. "Honestly, money was never one of the things I strived hard for. My dream growing up was to have a family and live with someone who cared about me as much as I cared about them. Yes, I know money makes life so much easier, but it doesn't bring happiness. Look at Gabriel, for one. He had money, but no matter how much he had, he wanted more."

"You seem to really like living on the ranch, and I love having you around. I hope you plan to stay close to us," Matilda added.

Lynn felt Bryson tense beside her. They hadn't talked about what she would do once the threat hanging over her head was gone. She would have no reason to stay at Montana Gold except to get to know Bryson more. *Would he want me to leave?*

As if he read her mind, he leaned over. "If you even think about leaving, Azadeh and I will follow you," he whispered.

"Hello, I'll be your waiter tonight. Can I get you guys something to drink?" their waiter asked. She appeared at the table at the right moment. Lynn didn't know how to answer Matilda's question without talking with Bryson first. She felt it would be better to have the conversation between just the two of them than in front of everyone.

Everyone at the table ordered a drink except Matilda, and when she said water, Noah smiled at her like he knew a secret. Lynn wanted to ask if she was pregnant but knew it wasn't her place. She would have to wait until the couple was ready to tell them. She wasn't the only one to pick up on the cue. Bryson smiled at her as if he knew the secret as well.

"I'll be right back with your drinks." The server turned and left the table.

"Has there been any more activity regarding Ricky?" Taz asked.

Bryson sighed. "I think Azadeh and I are in the clear. Ricky's operation is completely shut down, and his accounts are frozen. There would be no reason to come after me. As for Azadeh, it would cost too much money for them to try to get her. Next month she starts school."

"Can't wait," Azadeh added.

Each night, Bryson sat down with Azadeh and worked on math and English problems. He didn't want her to feel like she was behind or lost at school. Her uncle hadn't cared if she went to school or not, so she wasn't at the same level as other kids her age. It didn't seem to upset her. She worked hard each night, and when she did well, she got a chocolate bar at the end.

The rest of the night, they sat around the table,

laughing, and everyone talked about what they planned to do for Christmas. Lynn hoped she would still be with Bryson in a few weeks. She couldn't wait to watch Azadeh open gifts that were under the Christmas tree.

CHAPTER 13

Bryson sat across the breakfast table from Azadeh. She was shoving pancakes into her mouth as fast as she could. He had promised her he would never take her food away, but it didn't help. He'd spent the last few days trying to find her a therapist, and he'd finally found one. In a few days, she would sit down and talk with a licensed therapist. He liked that the man could speak to Azadeh in her native language. Sometimes he worried there was a disconnect between them because she didn't completely understand.

"Are you excited to go skating?"

"Uh-huh." It came out as a grumble because she still had food in her mouth.

Today was the first date with Azadeh and Lynn. Last night he'd wanted to stay up and talk with Lynn about her plans for the future, but when they were about to talk, Azadeh screamed from her room. It had been happening more frequently, so he was happy to finally have found a therapist. The nightmares worried him. She wasn't dealing with her trauma properly.

"You need to stick by Lynn's and my side at all times today." Bryson watched her every move, making sure she understood.

"Will Uncle be near?" Azadeh asked as she dropped her fork.

"No." Bryson was sure her uncle had given up. "Other people in the world are dangerous as well. I don't want you to get lost, because I'll be worried about you."

"I will stay by your side."

Bryson let out a breath. "Now that we have that settled, have you thought about what you want for Christmas?"

Azadeh stared at him with her pretty blue eyes. "A mom."

Bryson choked on the sip of coffee he'd taken. "I'm not sure I can find you a mom for Christmas. How about a new toy?"

Azadeh smiled up at him. "Lynn makes a good mom."

Bryson thought back to the time they'd shared in the spring. Lynn would make a great partner and mom, but that wasn't something he could make happen by Christmas. "I agree. Lynn would make a great mom, but I haven't dated her long enough to ask her."

"How long would you need to date?"

Bryson rubbed a hand down his face. This wasn't the conversation he'd planned to have with Azadeh. The sun had barely come up. "It's more of a feeling than a timeline."

Azadeh tilted her head. "I love her and you. Don't you have feelings for her?"

Bryson blinked a few times to stop the sheen in his eyes. This was the first time she'd told him she loved him. Bryson had known he loved the young girl the second she'd handed him the keys to the cuffs around his wrists. "You love me?"

She nodded. "And Lynn."

Bryson walked over and wrapped Azadeh in his arms. "I love you too," he whispered in her ear.

"Does that mean I can have Lynn as my mom?" Azadeh asked as she pulled out of his hug.

"Not yet. We have to wine and dine her until she never wants to leave us."

Azadeh pouted for a second before turning back. "You mean if I give her my doll, she might stay with us?"

Bryson brushed the hair from her eyes. "No, but going skating with her today is a start. Have you ever tried skating before?"

He needed to change the subject, just in case Lynn walked into the room. He knew Lynn loved the young girl, but he wanted her to like him just as much. The date today was the first one of many he had planned.

"No, but Lynn showed me a video online. I think I'm going to be good."

"I bet you will be." Bryson loved how Azadeh tried new things. She'd gone riding a few times, and he knew she would want a horse. Whenever they went somewhere, she would eye toys but never ask for one. Growing up, she didn't have money, and Bryson highly doubted her good-for-nothing uncle ever wanted to buy her a gift. In the coming months, when everything had settled down, he would get her something.

"Have you ever skated?"

"When I was younger, I would skate with Noah and my other brother, Grayson, in the winters. We had a large pond on our land that would freeze over during the winter. On the weekends, we would play hockey against each other."

"Will you teach me?" Azadeh asked before taking her dish to the sink.

"Yup."

She smiled back at him. He knew then he would do anything she wanted. Over the years, he'd heard about fathers being wrapped around their daughters' fingers. The statement had never registered with him before that moment.

Lynn watched as Bryson helped Azadeh lace up her skates. It was the middle of the day on a Wednesday, so the ice rink was empty. Lynn hadn't skated before, so she was happy she would only be making a fool out of herself in front of Bryson and Azadeh.

She couldn't hold back a smile over the conversation she had overheard. Lynn knew it was private, but when she heard her name, she couldn't help but listen. Azadeh had asked for a mom for Christmas, but it was more than that. She wanted Lynn to be her mom. It took everything in her not to burst into the kitchen and give the young girl exactly what she wanted. Bryson's voice was what had stopped her. She wanted to know how he felt.

When he'd said that he would have to woo her, her heart had opened a little more, and she turned to let the two continue their private conversation.

"Are you ready?"

"Yes," Lynn answered as she wobbled on her skates. She could barely walk on the padded ground, she had no clue how it was going to go when her feet hit the ice.

"I help you." Azadeh smiled up at her. "We learn together."

Lynn squeezed Azadeh's hand and steadied herself by grabbing onto Bryson's arm.

"TV makes this look so much easier."

Bryson's lips twitched for a second before he opened the gate to the ice rink. "You'll get the hang of it in no time. If not, you have padded pants on."

She didn't think her snow pants would have enough padding to protect her ass from hitting the hard ice.

Bryson held onto her hand as she stepped into the rink. "Hold onto the rails while I help Azadeh."

"Shit. I'm going to fall on my ass," Lynn said as she gripped the rail. Her feet slid in two different directions, neither of which she had planned for, and somehow she ended up on her ass. "I'm going to sit here for a second."

Laughter bubbled from Azadeh's throat. "You're silly."

"I'm going to take her around a few times, and then I'll be back to help you."

She nodded.

Bryson stood behind Azadeh and held her around the waist to catch her if she fell. By the second pass, Azadeh was skating on her own. Bryson hadn't left her side, even though she said she could do it on her own.

Seeing the two together brought tears to Lynn's eyes. Bryson was a good dad. Lynn only had a few memories with her dad, and the older she got, the more they faded away.

Azadeh continued to make her rounds around the

rink, and Bryson effortlessly skated over to Lynn, slowly stopping before he got too close.

His back straightened when he got close and noticed the tears in her eyes. "What's wrong? Did you hurt yourself when you fell?"

"Nothing's wrong." She reached up and wiped the tears from her eyes.

"Please tell me."

"I just never thought I would have this."

He nodded and reached down to offer her a hand. Lynn let out a breath, thankful that Bryson understood what she meant without having to explain it to him. When she was standing on wobbly legs, he pulled her into his arms and pressed a kiss to her lips. Not a soft one like he did from time to time. It was hard, with a purpose to show he felt the same way. Lynn felt a tug on her arm, and when she pulled back from Bryson and looked down, Azadeh stood next to them.

"Is this wooing?"

Bryson placed a quick kiss against Lynn's lips. "Yes," he said before scooping Azadeh up in his arms and taking off. He raced with her across the rink and spun for a second. Her laughter filled the air, and getting to see the girl so happy added a smile to Lynn's face.

Lynn wanted to be close to the two people she was in love with. Her feet scrambled for a second. She loved them both and didn't care how quickly their family happened. She just knew whatever the future brought, she wanted it to be with them. Now more than ever, she was determined to be next to them.

Not brave enough to skate without help, she held on to the side of the rink and worked her way to the other end, where Bryson was spinning Azadeh in circles.

"You made it over here. Why not try without your hands on the side now? It's similar to rollerblading, and you've done that in the past."

Lynn didn't think it was like rollerblading at all. She felt like a fish out of water, but she wanted to be next to the people she had come to care about in a short time. With a deep breath, she let go of the side and made slow progress toward the two. She took her time, not caring if a turtle could've passed her. When she was an arm's length from them, her feet stopped cooperating, but she wasn't going down alone that time.

She reached out and grabbed Bryson's arm. It caught him off guard, and they tumbled down together. Azadeh joined them on the ice. They were all laughing.

"Who wants some hot chocolate?"

Azadeh jumped up. "Me!" And she took off, skating toward the exit.

Bryson quickly yelled for her to wait for them. They needed to get back to the other side, and Lynn didn't have faith she could get there without falling a few more times.

After ten minutes of trying to get back up, Lynn finally stood on two feet.

Bryson grinned at her. "Do you want me to help? Or do you think you can get over there on your own?"

She glared up at him and grabbed his arm. "You can help me."

They skated together to the other side. Snow started to fall around them. It was like a scene straight out of a movie. Bryson stopped her in the middle of the ice and captured her lips. She wrapped her arms around him and pulled him in closer.

He pulled back and rested his forehead against hers. "What are you doing to me?" he whispered.

"The same thing you're doing to me. Now let's go get Azadeh some hot chocolate."

Bryson went up to the counter and got three hot chocolates while Lynn sat with Azadeh. The day was perfect, and Lynn wouldn't have wanted to spend it with anyone else.

"Do you like Bryson?"

The question took Lynn by surprise. She looked over to where Bryson was getting their drinks. "Yes, why?"

Azadeh shrugged her shoulders. "He likes you."

Before Lynn could ask anything else, Bryson

walked over and handed drinks to Azadeh and Lynn. "What were you guys talking about?"

Azadeh looked up at him. "Nothing." She took a sip of her hot cocoa before setting it to the side. "Can I go skate again?"

Bryson nodded, and she went back out on the ice. Bryson wrapped his arm around Lynn's shoulders as they watched Azadeh do a few laps around the rink.

Lynn leaned over and whispered, "You're getting lucky tonight."

CHAPTER 14

"How was your session with Doctor Reeder?" Lynn asked as she helped Azadeh put on her jacket.

The young girl sighed. "He wants to talk about bad things too much."

Bryson and the doctor had talked about what Azadeh needed to focus on to help her get rid of the nightmares. She saw him twice a week, and that was her third time going. Bryson wanted to come with her, but Noah had needed help with something, so he'd stayed back.

Lynn was enjoying the girls' trip to Bozeman with Azadeh. She planned to spend some time shopping with Azadeh so they could buy a gift for Bryson. She wasn't sure what to get him quite yet but hoped it would pop out when they were at the store.

"I know you don't like talking about your past, but you haven't had a nightmare since you started."

Azadeh scrunched her nose for a second. "You're right." She grabbed Lynn's hand. "Do you think Bryson will send me back if my nightmares continue?"

"To the doctor?"

"No, to my uncle."

"Nope, you're stuck with him for the rest of your life."

"And you?"

Lynn kneeled and wrapped her arms around the young girl. "You're never going to get rid of me. You're stuck with me for life too."

"Good. Can we go to the store now?"

Lynn grabbed the girl's hand, and they walked out of the doctor's office. It was near the mall, so it was easy to walk across the street to find a Christmas present for Bryson.

As they entered the mall and walked by the first store, Azadeh let out a squeal. "Can we get one?"

Lynn looked at the puppy in the window and debated buying it for a second, but she knew it wasn't the right time. They had so many things to figure out before buying another animal. "How about we take a picture and show it to Bryson and let him know you want a puppy?"

"Okay." Azadeh's attention quickly changed directions, and she was back to looking at the other stores. Lynn sighed in relief. She didn't know it would be that easy to distract Azadeh from the puppy. It wouldn't always be that easy, so she enjoyed it while she could.

Across the mall was a Western store that specialized in leatherwork. She grabbed Azadeh's hand. They walked across the middle of the mall to the other side. In the front of the store was a nice wallet. Images of Bryson's ratty old thing came to her mind.

An older gentleman sat behind the counter. "Hello, ladies."

"Hello. Do you do custom lettering on the wallets?"

"Yes, and we can add messages in the bottom right corner."

Lynn grabbed one of the wallets off the counter and turned it around in her hand. "How long would it take to add writing?"

He raised his glasses and took the wallet from her hand. "Depends on how much you want."

"Azadeh, do you want to put a special message in Bryson's gift?"

Azadeh nodded.

"Okay, what do you want it to say?"

"I love you, Dad."

Lynn hadn't heard Azadeh call Bryson dad yet. He would choke up when he saw the wallet, and she couldn't imagine getting him a better gift than one with a message from Azadeh.

"I can have that ready for you in ten minutes."

The two of them walked around the store,

looking at little figures as they waited for the gentleman to finish the wallet. It didn't take long before he was calling them over to look at it. Lynn ran her fingers across the special words and couldn't wait for Christmas Day, when Bryson opened his gift from Azadeh.

They spent another hour walking around the mall. Lynn bought Azadeh a toy horse and a beautiful Christmas dress. It was green and red with sparkles. Azadeh twirled around the store when she tried it on.

On their way out, matching pj's caught Lynn's eye, and she couldn't resist buying a set for the three of them. She had always wanted to wake up Christmas morning with matching pj's. She hoped Bryson would want to do the same. If not, she and Azadeh would match Christmas morning.

Lynn smiled as she glanced in the back seat. The car was filled with a few more bags than she had originally planned. It was the first time she had dipped into her new money, and she couldn't imagine spending it on anyone other than Azadeh.

Azadeh was quiet in the back seat, playing on her iPad. She loved that thing, and if they didn't watch her closely, she would spend hours watching American videos. Music was her favorite, and she had a pretty voice when she sang along to songs. Lynn had gotten used to being home with Azadeh each day. It would be strange when the young girl had to head to school.

Maybe Lynn needed to consider writing another program or seeing if she could find remote work. Lynn knew she wouldn't find a job as a programmer in Eagle Ridge. Leaving wasn't an option. Bryson and Azadeh had both wormed their way into her heart, and she couldn't imagine a day without them around.

She and Bryson had made love another time since the night in the cave. Each night, after tucking Azadeh into bed, Lynn would go to her own room until she knew everyone was asleep, then she would sneak across the hall to Bryson's room. She felt like a teenager hiding her secret boyfriend. In time, they would let Azadeh know they were getting closer.

Lynn turned off the main highway and headed toward the ranch. They weren't that far from home when she saw the BMW from the other day coming up close behind her. The hairs on the back of her neck stood up. The man didn't seem like the type to be around Eagle Ridge, and it seemed like he hadn't left. Lynn gripped the steering wheel as the car rode her back bumper. She slowed down and gave him room to move around her, but instead he got closer.

This time the man wasn't alone. She could see another person in the car. Her safest option was to keep driving and hope he would finally go around her. But instead, she felt his car tap her back bumper, and Azadeh's eyes met hers in the rearview mirror.

"I need you to listen to me," Lynn said.

Azadeh nodded.

"No matter what happens, I need you to run and hide."

"I won't—"

Her words were cut off when the car bumped the back of the truck again, this time a little harder.

Lynn pressed her foot on the gas. Maybe she could outrun him.

"You need to run. And when Bryson comes, tell him what happened."

The young girl had tears streaming down her face, and Lynn did everything in her power to try to stay under control.

The truck was going over eighty miles an hour when the car hit the back of them again. Lynn worried if she was going too fast, the crash would be really bad. She slowed down again and made sure her seat belt was tight. With a quick glance, she checked to make sure Azadeh had hers on.

"Hold on, Azadeh, and run the second the car stops."

The BMW hit the truck's fender, causing it to swerve, and when it turned, the tire caught the side of the road. Lynn tried to gather her wits. Azadeh's safety was her only concern. The young girl screamed when the car behind them struck again.

It was enough to send the truck into the ditch at the side of the road and roll. The sound of glass breaking made Lynn shield her face, and she hoped she and Azadeh wouldn't get cut. The truck flipped another time, as if in slow motion.

Azadeh's scream echoed through the cab. Lynn was sure her scream matched the young girl's. When the truck finally stopped, Lynn released her seat belt and fell from her seat. As quickly as possible, she went into the back seat and undid Azadeh's seat belt.

"Run." Lynn pointed to the window in the back. Each second was one second closer to them encountering the men who were after her.

Once she saw Azadeh squeeze out through the window, Lynn worked her way back into the front seat. Hopefully she could distract the men enough to let Azadeh escape.

A large hand pried the door open and pulled her out of the truck. "Look what we have here," the man snarled.

"I have money."

"I'm going to make your boyfriend pay for messing with me."

Lynn closed her eyes for a second. This must be Ricky. He wasn't after her. He just wanted revenge, and he was too chicken to go after Bryson. He had to use her to get to him.

He shoved her to the side and crouched back down. "Where's the girl?"

"What girl?"

Ricky walked over and grabbed her around the

neck, cutting off her air supply. The edges of her vision turned black from the lack of oxygen.

"Hey, we need to go."

"I want the girl too."

The other man fidgeted. "We don't have time. If someone comes along, you'll lose her too."

Ricky dropped his hands from Lynn's neck. She leaned over and coughed. Movement to her left caught her eye. She quickly shook her head, hoping Azadeh would stay hidden and not try to rescue her. Lynn didn't know what would happen if Ricky got his hands on the young girl. He had connections overseas and would probably try to send her back to her uncle. She hoped Bryson would be able to find Azadeh.

She didn't have time to catch her breath before Ricky dragged her across the cold snow toward the BMW. The front of the car was messed up from running into the truck. Lynn prayed it wouldn't start. Ricky took her to the back of the car and opened the trunk. When she didn't crawl in, he hit her on the back of the head, and everything went dark.

CHAPTER 15

"Have you heard from Lynn?" Noah asked.

They had just gotten back to the house with Grayson and Kara. Bryson had wanted to go with Lynn and Azadeh into town, but Lynn had insisted he help pick up his brother. She said she planned to take Azadeh shopping for a Christmas dress after her therapy session.

"No." He glanced down at his watch. They should have been on their way back by then, but he hadn't heard a thing.

Bryson walked toward the office and fired up his computer. Grayson followed behind and plopped down in the leather chair as Bryson booted up the laptop. Lynn had given him access to track her phone. He promised not to use it unless he felt like something was wrong, and his gut told him something was off. She always answered his texts, and if she was driving, Azadeh would answer for her. He'd been trying to get ahold of her for the past two hours.

The computer turned on, and he entered his password and clicked open the browser to pull up her location. Within seconds, he had it on the screen. He waited for the dot to move, but it never did. His truck was pulled over on the side of the road, not too far away.

His girls were in danger. He quickly opened another window and logged into the NSA satellite system. Once he had it positioned over the location, he zoomed in. His truck was on its side. Not wanting to waste another second, he jumped up from the chair and ran toward the door, his oldest brother on his heels.

"What's going on?" Noah called out. "Wait a second, and I'll come with."

"No, stay here in case they make it home, but they're in danger." Bryson grabbed Noah's keys from the counter and raced for the door with Grayson by his side.

Bryson took off out of the driveway, heading toward his truck. He hoped for once that his gut was wrong and they were okay.

Grayson didn't say a word next to him as he drove. The snow from the day before had been cleared from the roads, making it easy for him to speed and not worry about ice.

Waiting for a certain number of days to tell Lynn how he really felt seemed stupid. He wished she knew that he loved her more than anything. His heart squeezed in his chest thinking about what might've happened. Razor had promised him that Gabriel wouldn't come for her. *Did the man change his mind?*

Bryson pressed his foot down farther on the gas, wanting to get to her as fast as possible. In the distance, he could see the white truck lying in the ditch on its side. It looked worse in person than it did on the satellite feed he had pulled up.

When they neared the truck, he slammed on the brakes and slid to a stop. He placed the truck in park and jumped out, heading to where his women were. When he was halfway across the road, Grayson wrapped an arm around him.

"What the fuck?" he screamed at his brother.

Grayson didn't loosen his grip. "We can't go running in. What if they were taken? You could destroy any evidence we might find."

Bryson nodded. "I'll be careful." Grayson loosened his grip, and Bryson walked over to the edge to glance into the truck.

They weren't there. *What can I do now?* Bryson let out a bloodcurdling scream. Lynn and Azadeh were in danger. He stepped forward and heard a faint sniffle. Grayson stilled next to him, hearing the same thing. They both searched the area but couldn't see anyone.

"Azadeh, are you there?" Bryson shouted as loud as he could and waited for some sign, hoping the sound had come from her.

Out of the corner of his eye, he watched as the snow moved, revealing the young girl. Azadeh was okay. She had hidden under the snow. Not caring about anything other than getting to his girl, Bryson tore off after her and wrapped her in his arms, squeezing her so tight she tapped his back.

After a few seconds, he finally set her down and knelt in front of her. She looked from him to his brother. She hadn't met Grayson yet. "That is my brother Grayson. Do you know where Lynn is?"

Azadeh reached up and wiped her tears away. "He took her."

"Who?"

"The man who shot at us in Jalalabad."

Ricky had somehow gotten back into the country without him knowing. The only reason he would go after Lynn was if he knew how much she meant to him. Time was ticking, and they needed to find her before Ricky took her out of the country, or worse, killed her.

"Do you remember anything else?"

"Lynn made me promise to go and hide. She said you would come for me, but I didn't want the bad guy to get Lynn."

"I'm happy she made you hide. Did you do exactly what Lynn told you do?"

Azadeh shook her head. "I waited until they were gone to hide."

He should have been mad. She'd put herself in danger and hadn't completely listened to Lynn. In the future, they would need to explain the importance of hiding the second they told her to.

"Did you hear them say where they were taking her?"

"Yes."

"Where?" Grayson asked. He had his cell phone in hand, waiting for the information so he could let Noah know what was going on.

Bryson couldn't head into a fight with just Grayson and Azadeh by his side. He would need Azadeh to be safe before he went after the man who took Lynn.

"Hotel."

There was only one hotel in town. Bryson hoped that was where they planned to take her. Grayson was on the phone with Noah, calling for help. They would need to go back to the house to get guns and drop Azadeh off.

∽

BRYSON CROUCHED and watched the hotel room. He and his brothers had waited until dark to come for

Lynn. It would make the extraction easier, and it gave them time to run through everything. The front desk clerk had confirmed Ricky and another person were in the room. Bryson guessed it was someone Ricky had hired.

Azadeh was back at the ranch with Kara and Matilda. Hank had sent extra men to the house to keep watch in case Ricky tried something else. Grayson was posted at the back of the hotel to make sure Ricky couldn't escape that direction. Noah hid to one side of the door and Bryson to the other. Bryson approached the room and knocked hard on the door. "Housekeeping."

"Go away!" Ricky shouted back.

Not wanting to break the door down, Bryson knocked again, and when it cracked open, he pushed his way in, catching the man off guard. Bryson wrapped his arm around the man at the door and squeezed until the man passed out.

Bryson let him drop to the ground and scanned the room. Ricky stood next to Lynn with a gun to her head. His old teammate had changed over the last month and a half. His hair was greasy, and his clothes hung off his body. The size of his clothes wasn't what caught Bryson's attention though. It was that they were so dirty.

The smell was enough to make Bryson gag. "Let Lynn go. This is between you and me."

"You took everything from me." Ricky wiped his

arm across his face as he sniffled. Bryson hadn't realized Ricky had been doing drugs, but right then, Ricky looked like a man going through withdrawals.

Bryson didn't take his eyes off Ricky. He was worried if he looked at Lynn, he would lose his composure, and he had to stay calm if he was going to save her.

Out of the corner of his eye, movement caught his attention. Grayson had snuck into the hotel room from the back. If Bryson could keep Ricky talking, Grayson might be able to take Ricky out from behind.

"What do you want, Ricky?"

"I want you to pay for taking everything from me. Do you know what happens when Ibrahim al-Asiri doesn't get his drugs?"

"No."

Ricky lifted his shirt to show his chest. It was covered in scars. Pus oozed from the wounds, and Bryson realized where Ricky's stench was coming from. "This." He pressed the gun harder into Lynn's temple. "Get me the girl, and I will leave. Ibrahim said if I bring her back, my debt will be erased."

Bryson closed his eyes for a second. "Not going to happen."

Ricky cocked back his arm holding the gun, but before Bryson could react, he slammed it down on Lynn's head. The cry that escaped her lips broke his heart. Ricky didn't have time to react again.

Grayson had come up behind him and pinned his arms.

Noah grabbed the gun out of Ricky's hand. The urge to beat the shit out of him was strong, but Lynn needed Bryson more. His brothers quickly took Ricky and his lacky out of the room, and Bryson dropped to the floor in front of Lynn. He untied her hands and feet. When her eyes didn't open, he ran to the bathroom and got a clean rag and soaked it with water.

He rushed back and wiped her forehead. Her eyes fluttered open, and she glanced around the room. "Azadeh?"

"She's fine and at the house with Kara and Matilda."

Lynn let out her breath and rested her head against his chest. "I was so worried they would find her."

Bryson kissed the top of her head. "Thank you for protecting our daughter."

Lynn nodded against his chest. The next two hours they spent talking to the cops. Local police would hold Ricky until someone from the CIA could deal with him. Ricky wouldn't spend his time in a normal jail. He would be taken to a place nobody knew about and pumped for information.

The man who'd helped Ricky was a thug for hire and would end up serving a few years for kidnapping. Bryson was happy that everyone who had been hunting them was finally locked away. He didn't worry about Gabriel coming after them because Antonio was already working on taking over the whole Rockefeller company.

"Ready to head home?" he asked.

"Yes."

He leaned down and captured Lynn's lips. She wrapped her arms around his neck and pulled him in closer. Bryson swiped his tongue across her lips, demanding entrance. Time stopped around them. He pulled back and placed a kiss on her nose. "I love you, Lynn."

She smiled up at him. "I love you." She brushed her lips across his. "Thank you for saving me. Now I want to go see Azadeh."

EPILOGUE

CHRISTMAS DAY

Bryson pulled Lynn closer, leaned down, and placed a kiss on her lips. A week had passed since Ricky had kidnapped her. Bryson still worried every time she insisted on running into town alone, but he knew it wasn't rational to place her in a room and throw away the key.

He had a surprise for her, and he hoped she would like it. Over the past week, they had talked about their future. Lynn loved working with animals and didn't want to move back to the city. They had talked about looking for a ranch close to Montana Gold. Noah and Matilda were happy staying in Montana and didn't plan to leave.

The night before, when Lynn had gone to read Azadeh a bedtime story, he'd sat and had a glass of whiskey with his two brothers. Grayson told them that he and Kara were thinking about moving back to Montana. They liked Denver, but Grayson wanted to be closer to his brothers.

"Did you have fun talking with your brothers last night?"

"Yes." Bryson's lips twitched. "But it wasn't easy putting together that dollhouse after a couple of glasses of whiskey."

Lynn rolled her eyes. "Did you at least use all the parts?"

Noah had insisted it would be easy when they'd ordered it online. Bryson could've paid to have it put together. Last night while the brothers were talking about the future, they'd worked on the house.

"Most of the parts. Then we added a few of our own."

"I know for a fact that the house came with instructions. I bet you guys didn't even open them."

Nope. They hadn't touched them. Another one of Noah's bright ideas, thinking they didn't need help. By the time they'd halfway put it together, it was too late to try figuring out where they'd gone wrong.

Bryson pressed his lips to hers again. "I don't want to talk about that dollhouse. I want to kiss my girlfriend."

Lynn gently pushed at his chest. "Everyone is already up, and I want to see Azadeh's face when she opens her gifts."

"Fine," Bryson grumbled. "I do have a question for

you before we head downstairs. I don't want you to be caught off guard by Grayson."

Lynn nibbled her lip. "Okay."

"Grayson and Kara are planning to move back to Montana. They want all of us to live on the farm. They're giving Noah and me each a section of the land so we can build our own houses out here. What do you say?"

"You want me to move in with you?"

"Yes."

Lynn looked toward the door and back to him. "Do you think Azadeh is okay with that?"

"We both want you to live with us. If Azadeh had it her way, we would be married tomorrow and giving her a brother or sister a week later."

Each day at breakfast with Azadeh, before Lynn came down, Azadeh would ask if he and Lynn had dated long enough. Bryson told her the same thing each morning. "It takes longer than a few days." Bryson already knew he would marry Lynn, but he wanted her to enjoy life and have fun.

Not too far in the future, he would love to see her belly swell with his kids. He couldn't wait until the whole family had houses nearby and their kids could grow up together. Bryson knew Azadeh would be the ringleader and keep them in line.

He heard the pitter-patter of feet running down the hallway before the bedroom door burst open. Azadeh had on a pair of red Christmas pj's. Under the covers, Bryson had matching pants on, and Lynn wore a matching set. The three were primed for their first Christmas together as a family.

Azadeh ran toward the bed and jumped in, climbing between Bryson and Lynn. "Santa came last night."

"Really?"

"Yes, tons of presents under the tree."

Bryson smiled at Lynn. "Is everyone else up?"

"Yes. Uncle Noah told me to tell you it was time to get up."

Bryson jumped out of bed, picked Azadeh up, and twirled her in the air. Her laughter filled the room and his heart with so much joy.

"Let's go see what Santa brought us."

Bryson shifted Azadeh to his hip, and Lynn grabbed his hand. The three headed down the stairs to spend their first of many Christmases together.

When they reached the bottom stair, Noah was down on one knee, proposing to Matilda. Bryson watched as she kept a protective hand on her stomach. Noah had told them last night that they were expecting, and Grayson had followed with the same surprise.

Their family kept growing, and he loved every moment of it.

The End!

ALSO BY LINZI BAXTER

White Hat Security Series

Hacker Exposed

Royal Hacker

Misunderstood Hacker

Undercover Hacker

Hacker Revelation

Hacker Christmas

Hacker Salvation

Nova Satellite Security Series
(White Hat Security Spin Off)

Pursuing Phoenix

Pursuing Aries - March 31, 2020

Immortal Dragon

The Dragon's Psychic

The Dragon's Human

The Dragon's Mate - February 25, 2020

Montana Gold (Brotherhood Kindle World)

Grayson's Angel

Noah's Love

Bryson's Treasure

A Flipping Love Story (Badge of Honor World)

Unlocking Dreams

Unlocking Hope

Unlocking Love - May 2020

Siblings of the Underworld

Hell's Key

Hell's Future

Hell's Vacation 2020

Visit linzibaxter.com for more information and release dates.

Join Linzi Baxter Newsletter at Newsletter

ABOUT LINZI BAXTER

Linzi Baxter lives in Orlando, Florida with her husband and lazy basset hound. She started writing when voices inside her head wouldn't stop talking until the story was told. When not at work as an IT Manager, Linzi enjoys writing action-packed romances that will take you to the edge of your seat.

She enjoys engaging her readers with strong, interesting characters that have complex and stimulating stories to tell. If you enjoy a little (or maybe a whole lot) of steam and spice, don't miss checking out White Hat Security series.

When not writing, Linzi enjoys reading, watching college sports (GO UCF Knights), and traveling to Europe. She loves hearing from her readers and can't wait to hear from you!

Sign up for Linzi Baxter's VIP Club for the latest news, giveaways, experts, and more.

It's completely free to sign up, and I will never spam you. It's easy to opt out at any time.

Click here to sign up!

facebook.com/authorlinzibaxter

twitter.com/authorbaxter

instagram.com/authorlinzibaxter

BROTHERHOOD PROTECTORS

ORIGINAL SERIES BY ELLE JAMES

Brotherhood Protectors Series
Montana SEAL (#1)
Bride Protector SEAL (#2)
Montana D-Force (#3)
Cowboy D-Force (#4)
Montana Ranger (#5)
Montana Dog Soldier (#6)
Montana SEAL Daddy (#7)
Montana Ranger's Wedding Vow (#8)
Montana SEAL Undercover Daddy (#9)
Cape Cod SEAL Rescue (#10)
Montana SEAL Friendly Fire (#11)
Montana SEAL's Mail-Order Bride (#12)
SEAL Justice (#13)
Ranger Creed (#14)
Delta Force Strong (#15)
Montana Rescue (Sleeper SEAL)
Hot SEAL Salty Dog (SEALs in Paradise)
Hot SEAL Hawaiian Nights (SEALs in Paradise)

ABOUT ELLE JAMES

ELLE JAMES also writing as MYLA JACKSON is a *New York Times* and *USA Today* Bestselling author of books including cowboys, intrigues and paranormal adventures that keep her readers on the edges of their seats. With over eighty works in a variety of sub-genres and lengths she has published with Harlequin, Samhain, Ellora's Cave, Kensington, Cleis Press, and Avon. When she's not at her computer, she's traveling, snow skiing, boating, or riding her ATV, dreaming up new stories. Learn more about Elle James at www.ellejames.com

Website | Facebook | Twitter | GoodReads | Newsletter | BookBub | Amazon

Follow Elle!
www.ellejames.com
ellejames@ellejames.com

facebook.com/ellejamesauthor
twitter.com/ElleJamesAuthor